not so common people

t gamache

Live. Love. Music.

Not Always in that Order

INDIEOWL
PRESS

4700 Millenia Blvd
Ste 175 #90776
Orlando, FL 32839

info@indieowlpress.com
IndieOwlPress.com

not so common people

Cover Design & Interior Layout by NightOwlFreelance.com

Paperback ISBN-13: 978-1-949193-86-2

To all the songs played through headphones saving lives all over the world.

Contents

not so common people

Prologue

Some people call it a collection. Others call it an obsession. I call it my past. My present. My life. It's the reason why I don't understand or relate to most people. But, honestly, it's just 2,137 vinyl records...stored in alphabetical order.

You see, I'm an avid record collector and quite possibly the first person afflicted with Constant Music Syndrome—it's a real thing that I just made up. I live, breathe, and sleep music. If I'm not listening to it, I'm reading about it or watching live bands. (I do that mostly online, as I hate crowds.) Going to shows results in a small panic-attack every time. Welcome to being me.

I received a Bachelor's degree in Music Performance, but I just wanted to study Rock and Roll History. Not much money in that, as you can imagine, so now I spend my time lost in my music and make a living just to support my habit and resign myself to becoming anomalous to the human existence.

The collection is mostly a reflection of my life and personality. Well, some of it is. If I were to pull out my favorites and line them up on a wall, you would see who I was. The Smiths, The Beatles, various Britpop bands would live there. But there are also the countless albums I've purchased because I'm "supposed" to. You know, the "classics" that are on every *Rolling Stone* and Billboard list of all-time "greatest" records, but you don't actually give a crap about them.

I'll give you an example: The Rolling Stones, *Exile on Main Street*. Considered by many to be one of the greatest albums of all time, but to me it's a bunch of blah blah blah. I've never been a huge fan. This is nothing against the supposed writing genius of Jagger/Richards, but they are just not my thing. Yet, I purchase the album because, as any self-proclaimed rock music junkie and wannabe musician, I'm supposed to own it and understand it.

But I don't. Sometimes I just fake it really well.

My personal life mirrors this. I have some great relationships with folks who totally "get" me, and then there is the rest of the world. I fake it with them, and I only hang out with them because I'm "supposed to," but I don't really get them. I say "supposed to" because they are family.

My older brother, Graham, is a self-made lots-of-moneyaire who buys and sells crap. I don't even know what exactly he buys and sells because it's so painfully boring; I stopped listening to his tales of career triumphs five years ago.

My other brother, Calvin, is a Lutheran minister. He's also older than me but younger than Graham. Why he's a Lutheran when we were raised Catholic, I have no idea, but I have even less in common with him than I do with Graham, if that is even possible.

My younger sister, Marcie, is a housewife with three kids (my oldest nephew and a set of twin boys), and we can just stop there. I have yet to produce a progeny, so I have no clue how she even exists from day to day. I mean, have you ever met a kid? I never thought it was humanly possible to have so many needs at one time. Watching my first nephew when he was just an infant, you would have thought the world was ending. (Admittedly, I was praying for that very thing to happen—and if truth be told, I think my brother-in-law was as well.) The way my nephew screamed to be fed! *What the hell?* At first, I felt bad for Joe (my brother-in-law), but he continued to procreate with my sister, so my sympathy-well dried up.

My parents are wonderful folks who really do try to understand, but somehow, they look at me with a glazed-over expression, only barely hiding the fact that they are concerned I was somehow switched at birth.

I'm sure that this is all *extremely* interesting to you, but you're the one who started reading, so here we go.

My name is Nathan Smythe—pronounced Smith. (My family gave me the annoying burden of having the easiest name on the planet, yet I have to tell everyone how to spell it—it's wonderful.)

I live in a great apartment with my roommates, Claire and Frank, in the College Park section of Orlando. The three of us have a wonderfully platonic relationship (Frank is gay, and Claire and I could never date…eww.) Orlando is not the Disney-fied city most think it is, but we'll get to its coolness later. I was born in Rhode Island and went to school in Pittsburgh, where I met Claire. How did we end up in Florida, you ask? My parents moved here when I was in college and slowly my siblings and I have all gravitated south. I don't know why because Florida can be hell on earth, but still, here I am. Claire joined me because she was running away from a psychopathic ex-boyfriend, and who better to move in with than her music-obsessed introvert friend? And there's nothing that makes me feel better than the thought of an Alpha Male lunk looking for his lost love as she seeks exile in my apartment. Well, that's what Frank is for I guess. The great gay protector. I feel so masculine.

I work as a barista in a local café. (I know, could I be more of a hipster?) Claire is a bank-teller and Frank is a freelance photographer and workout fanatic. We may seem like we have little in common, but the thing we all share is our love for music. We each spend way too much time and money following our passion. Last year, Claire and I flew to LA to see Morrissey because he refused to come to the

Sunshine state. Frank was not pleased.

"If anyone deserves to see the Pope of Mope and possibly the greatest gay icon of our time, shouldn't it be me?" Frank lamented.

"I cannot afford to pay for your ticket, and you just told me you were out of town for the month of June visiting Gary's family in Nova Scotia—stop your whining! I didn't write his tour schedule and it was the only date left. Claire's cousin is putting us up and Graham is letting me borrow his miles for the flights," I told him while he tried not to burn the vegetarian pizza he was reheating.

"If you want to cancel your plans, you're welcome to come along— but the last time you skipped out on meeting Gary's family, you didn't hear the end of it, which means I didn't either. I'm not going to be responsible for another month of misery from the two of you," I reminded him.

"Just let me complain. You know I don't mean it, but I'm going to say it anyway, so you might as well just let me get it out. Gary's family, especially his mom, are huge pains-in-the-ass, but I think we are going to break the news to them that we are planning on getting married. Even though we have been together for-e-ver, I think that some of them still don't know we are a *thing*."

I looked at him with a raised eyebrow. "Maybe that's because you refuse to move in together, and the only time the two of you act like a couple is in front of Claire and I. You're as scared of being affectionate in public as he is. Why, I'm not sure? Half of our friends are open, and their families have come around, but you two still live like it's 1986."

That was the last we spoke of the Morrissey show, but it gives you an idea of how the three of us relate. But now, I need to travel to see my family and spend the Thanksgiving holiday with them. It's like a small, torture-filled day. Graham will belittle me, Calvin will preach to me, and Marcie & Joe will wonder when and if I'm ever going to join them in the "wonderful" world of married life. They are convinced that Claire and I are the perfect couple but, honestly, I could marry Marcie easier, or even Frank for that matter. I love Claire, but the fact is, we are exactly alike, which is why we are perfect friends but terrible romantic partners.

I will drive across town to Graham's house in the Dr. Phillips neighborhood, which is a grotesquely large McMansion that he occupies with his flavor of the month, currently Janine. I'm sure she is a wonderful person, but as much trouble as I have relating to my family, I have even more issues with the girls Graham dates. They are usually a combination of mannequin and stripper, where the mannequin has the better personality.

Yes, I know, I'm an arrogant, difficult, artsy whiner. But it's my life and my story, so hang on.

Chapter 1

holiday bliss

Claire joins me for the holiday at Graham's because her parents still live in Pittsburgh, and she has no desire to travel this November. Beyond the love of music that we share, we are also the self-proclaimed black sheep of our families. We love them all, and we realize that we are the strange ones, as they seem to relate to each other and get along just fine. But that doesn't stop us from living in the shame of who we are: audiophile music junkies who use every waking minute and dollar supporting our addiction. I will someday figure out how to maneuver through normal, "big-people" talk, but for now I surround myself with like-minded souls.

As we pull into Graham's driveway, I remember again how nice his place is. I've got to admit he's done well, seems a little much for one guy, but to each his own. It's like Claire is reading my mind.

"I realize every time I come here how ridiculous Graham's house is.

I mean, for a single guy…who would want to clean that much house?" Claire wondered out loud.

"He doesn't," I reminded her. "He hires out for all his crap. Food delivery, grocery delivery, house cleaner, pool dude. I don't think he's lifted a finger to maintain any of this place since he's moved in. Basically, he works so he doesn't have to work."

I thought it was funny, but the humor was lost on Claire as she just stared as we got out of my Civic and walked past his latest Tesla purchase. Approaching the door, I noticed that we were the last to arrive. I hated being first, but sometimes—with my family, being last was just as bad. Always the one on display, never the wallflower, like I preferred.

"What up, Van Halen!" Graham said, smacking me on the ass as we walked through his huge front door. Two things I couldn't stand: overly hyper male touching and being called a washed-up hair-band metal guitarist. I have always wanted to think of myself as more like *The Smith's*, Johnny Marr, than Eddie VH, but that comparison would be lost on Graham. Since I was a music major, and wasn't making money with my degree, he liked to use a thinly-veiled insult every time he saw me. My lifestyle was not to his liking, and he never let me forget it.

"How's the coffee bar business treating ya? I stopped in there the other day for a Pumpkin Spice and was going to say hi, but you weren't working. You didn't get fired, did you?"

Wow—insulted again in a matter of 30-seconds. Please don't come visit me, is all I could think, but the response came out somewhat nicer. "No, still employed, but I've never worked at Starbucks, if that's what you're thinking. I work at Foxtail," I, gently and without a trace of sarcasm, reminded him.

"Really, that's a place? Foxtail? Sounds like a strip-club. Sorry, Claire—good to see you, by the way. Happy Thanksgiving!" Graham was already not paying attention to us.

"Thanks, Graham, good to see you, too." Claire smirked and shot me a glance somewhere between compassion and ridicule.

We made our way through the labyrinth that was his foyer to the living room. I found my dad and Calvin in a discussion that had all the trappings of something to be avoided. My father had become a devout agnostic, convincing my mom that going to church was a waste of their time now that they were retired.

"Why would we want to tie ourselves to any type of schedule, Joan?" Dad would say. Mom finally saw it his way, and they have not stepped into a church in years. I think my mother prayed for her children more than anything else when we all attended services weekly anyway.

"Dad, you really need to hear what the Lord is doing in the world today, and that may require you to step back into a house of worship." Calvin was putting on his pastor voice, which spoke in slower and lower tones than his normal voice. "We are all sinners, Dad. Just some of us deal with it differently."

"Nathan & Claire! Good to see you! So glad you could make it, Claire. Nathan is so much happier when you are around," Dad announced as we entered the room. I don't know if my dad was more relieved to see that Claire had accompanied me or that he could end his conversation with Calvin.

"Thanks, Mr. Smythe, it's always a pleasure. And if you remember our kitchen, we could use a good meal."

"Please, call me Jim, and yes my son doesn't seem to be the best chef in the world." Dad laughed.

"There are three of us who live there, Dad. Not sure when I became the sole food provider." (I knew he was joking. It was a way that my father and I could relate to each other.)

My dad had been a successful lawyer in town and was recently retired, but he always seemed to hate what he did for a living for as long as I could remember. He spent his spare time doting on my mother and building model ships with very intricate sailing mechanisms. It was his escape. This I could relate to as well.

He chuckled as he stood to embrace both Claire and me. The smell of food wafted from the kitchen, and I could hear Marcie and my mother in there doing something.

"Hello there," I said as we made our way to Graham's kitchen that was the size of most people's living rooms. Marcie, Joe, and Mom were plating food and loading up the side dishes. It seemed like we had made it just in time; dinner was about to be served.

"Nate! Happy Thanksgiving!!" My sister insisted on calling me Nate, even though I was never really a Nate, but it was okay coming from her.

"Hey, Nate," Joe said, carrying out a platter full of turkey to the table barely missing my sister on the way. "Watch out, hon, I'm right behind you."

My sister moved without saying anything, inching closer to me and Claire. Joe was a nice guy, but my sister seemed to be giving him the cold shoulder recently. Didn't really seem fair, but she was always stressed about something involving the kids.

"Hey, Claire, good to see you," she said. "Can you give me a hand for a sec?" And with that Marcie and Claire disappeared. I knew what was coming and felt bad for Claire already. Marcie was going to gather her kids who were in the back family room, probably on Uncle Graham's Xbox 1 (although I don't think you can put a five-year-old and two three-year-old's on an Xbox, so they are probably just chewing on the controllers, unless she actually brought their toys, which is highly doubtful—this is Marcie we are talking about. Not Mother-of-the-Year material). Claire was about as comfortable around kids as I was, but oh well, sucked to be her. You know, sometimes a free meal comes with a price.

"Happy Thanksgiving, Mom," I said, walking over and giving her a hug. Mom was getting old and these holidays meant the world to her. She knew her kids were all on different planets but loved when we were all under one roof.

"Well, Happy Stuffed-Bird-Day to you, too, Nathan." She smiled and hugged back. That's Mom's nickname for Thanksgiving; she has used it for all the years I can remember.

"Where's Janine?" I inquired, not really caring, but thought I'd be nice.

"Oh, well, seems she's a thing of the past, according to Graham. She wanted to settle down and get too serious for him, I guess."

Mom could convince herself of anything when it came to her kids, but she knew deep down that he was bored—or found some new arm-candy on one of his recent business outings—and it would only be a matter of time before we had to endure a new bimbo.

With that, Graham walked in and picked up on our conversation. "Yeah, no putting a saddle on this stallion! She needed to hit the road, and I figured no time better than before the holidays. I'll be damned if I'm gonna pay for a Christmas present for that...chick." He was obviously censoring himself in front of Mom. Not that Janine was a bitch, but Graham always referred to his ex's as bitches—since that's what they must have been if they were not good enough to be with him, right?

Well, there you have it, Graham's collection of women is starting to rival my LP list, but I'm guessing that most of his will not stand the test of time as well as *Abbey Road*.

Dinner was served and it was wonderful as always. The conversation stayed mostly civil, without many snide comments.

"You mentioned that Dad has seen your kitchen," Calvin said. "You know, I've never been invited to see your place."

His guilt knows no bounds, and here I thought it was confined to Sundays.

"No time like the present—why don't you come over for dinner sometime? We would love that," Claire replied without even running it by me first.

Ugh. This is why we could never get married.

"You know, next week is kinda light in the church schedule. I could stop over on Tuesday or Wednesday, if that works for you guys? I'll bring dessert. What do you think, Nathan?"

I could be honest and say that sounds like a horrible idea, but I chose, "Sure, Tuesday is better for me cuz I work Wednesday, and you could meet Frank. He leaves for Portland later in the week, so let's go with Tuesday."

I could almost feel Mom smiling as her children interacted without her having to initiate the conversation. But, truth be told, Calvin had been invited before but declined because he thought that Claire and I were "living in sin." Now that we have finally convinced him that a man and a woman *can* actually live together without there being any carnal activity, he'd decided that visiting for dinner was a "great" idea. I don't think he quite has a handle on Frank's lifestyle, but one hurdle at a time.

The rest of the conversation was fine, not great, but harmless at least. Which, looking back on holidays past, is a welcomed change, believe it or not. Graham regaled us with tales of voyages and deals so exciting I almost had a clue about what he did for a living. I know I sound jaded against my brother, and I am. But, to be fair, he's a dick. Not just in his braggadocio but in the way he treats people. I know I haven't given a positive impression of the women he's dated, but Janine was actually the closest to a real person we've ever seen him with and he's dumped her for basically no reason. This is his track-record, though: they move in with him and then are tossed aside. He doesn't even seem to care about how that can turn somebody's head upside down. You commit then you quit. So, I kinda feel like I have reason to piss in his oatmeal.

Calvin stayed quiet for the most part and politely chuckled at the right moments in Graham's diatribe (a trick I wish I could learn). Usually, Calvin rambles on about his congregation and how we would do well with a visit to his church. Recently, though, he mentioned that he's been venturing beyond the pulpit and making some friends outside his church. This is great because—if I could let you in on a secret— I've been scared for Calvin. He's been a loner ever since finding God sometime in his third year at Rollins College here in Orlando. He had been a philosophy major up to that point. (If you think my music degree is useless, I was the "crown jewel" while he was studying philosophy.) And then something happened. The next thing we know, he's all, "I'm going to be a preacher pastor person..." He'd had only a few friends at school and even less as he'd gotten older. He would mention getting out from time to time, but there have been no "bros" in my bro's life.

Mom and Dad casually mentioned they were taking off on a road trip starting next week that was going to take them through the new year. *What the hell?* That means they'll be skipping town…for Christmas? Don't get me wrong, they can do whatever floats their boat, but Dad has NEVER wanted us to spend the holidays apart, and now here he goes taking off to freaking Vancouver in the middle of winter!? Who's going to cook Christmas dinner? I am *not* going to be one of those guys who ends up at Denny's on Christmas because his mother all of sudden thinks she's all highfalutin and is going to deprive her offspring of their holiday feast! *Oh, for the love...*

"Hey, that sounds great!" says Graham. "You guys deserve to get away for a while. We'll be fine, but you have to at least FaceTime us opening presents."

I smile as I imagine myself punching Graham in the face.

"We will hold dinner at our house!" Joe interjects, "We've been wanting to have everyone over, and that is the perfect time—right, hon?"

I smile as I imagine Marcie punching Joe in the face.

"Sure," she says, looking like she's contemplating cooking Joe and serving him for dinner.

"Well, that's settled! Dinner at the Donovan's house!" Joe exclaims, not even noticing that his wife is less than thrilled. *How did they have three kids?*

Claire mentions that she won't be traveling at that time either, and Marcie seems relieved that she'll be joining us. I ask if it's okay for Frank to tag along, as I know that Gary is out of town since Frank had *repetitively* mentioned it recently.

Dinner concludes with more polite conversation, and Claire and I are finally able to excuse ourselves around 7 p.m.

"Thank you for coming," I say on the drive home. "It's exhausting for me every year, but somehow having an ally in the house makes it a little more enjoyable. Although, *what the hell were you thinking* inviting my brother over for dinner next Tuesday? You do realize I don't like him that much, right? I mean, he's blood and all, but I would think twice about giving him a kidney—or any extra body part, for that matter."

"Shut up, Nathan. Calvin is a lost soul, and if you can't see that, well, doom on you. He needs people to talk to and socialize with or he is going to just get more depressed."

"Yes, I realize he needs people to talk to. I just don't want to be *those* people. He has a warped way of looking at the world, and volunteering to spend time listening to him just seems emotionally masochistic."

Although I'm driving, I can feel Claire looking at me with disgust. "This coming from the man who views life through the needle of a turntable and whose everyday mood is determined by the playlist he selected for his drive to work. Shall I remind you of the tantrum you pulled because our record shop accidentally sold your copy of *The Queen is Dead* box set? *That* is a man who has a "warped" sense of the world, my dear."

I could see that this conversation was now over. How could I possibly continue to talk to her about Calvin's messed up philosophy on life when she can't even comprehend how important and life changing *The Smiths* album reissue was!? I mean, c'mon! This was a 5 LP box set with a 2017 remaster of the album, additional tracks, B-sides and the infamous "Live in Boston" recording! What was there not to understand!? How could you *not* lose your mind!? And don't give me they "accidentally" sold it, no, that moron Rick at Rock n Roll Heaven (my local record shop) knew exactly what he was doing. I'd pissed him off when I told him his record store was "little more than a second-rate pawn shop" because they didn't have one in stock on the release day and I had to special order it. And then he sold it to the first cute girl who walked into his pathetic store. The exact same store I still frequented on a weekly basis, by the way. *Whatever.*

The rest of the ride was pretty quiet as I tried to think of ways to get appendicitis by Tuesday and avoid the whole thing. I figured the next best thing I could do was to have Frank cook one of his awful vegetarian meals.

Ah, who am I kidding? Frank's a great cook and will love the idea of entertaining my one "bro" he's never met.

Chapter 2

the monday after

So, after my turkey coma on Thursday, I basically spent the weekend avoiding every retail outlet and the masses of parents striving to receive the Perfect Parent Award by acquiring the most amazing toys on the planet for their spoiled children. (I swear I'm really not that cynical.) I really do like some people. I also lost myself in the making of a new playlist that would get my mental state ready for the upcoming visit of my oh-so-righteous brother.

Let me say a thing or two about playlists. It's the modern version of the "mix-tape." The thing about a playlist for a vinyl aficionado such as myself is they're like junk food for the musical soul. You put together a mix-tape or a playlist so that you don't have to think about what you're listening to. The thinking has already been done. Basically, what you're saying is, "Don't challenge me with music that I may have to decide if I like or not, just make it sweet to my ears." While this is fine for a road trip or getting on one of those self-torture devices found in gyms and other places where sweaty people hang out, they are not how I prefer to enjoy my music. You see, the thing about vinyl is that it is not made to be mindless and easy. You can't just touch your iPhone and the perfect playlist comes out. You have to take the record out, smell it (well, you don't *have* to smell it, that's just something I do, but you *should*), then place the disc on the platter and put the needle onto the first groove. And then, when side one has ended, you have to flip it over and begin the process again for side two. There is no skipping tracks, there is no pausing your music to answer your phone. It is an experience. Preferably done with headphones. Not to be rushed. Ahhh...and this is why I don't have many friends.

As I began listening to my "It's a New Morning" playlist on my way to work Monday, I realized, once again, how music can save your life. I lost myself in the tunes I knew by heart and that took me to a place of serene aural beauty. Sometimes, I am amazed that I haven't caused more vehicular damage as I tend to get really lost in the songs, remembering what album, which track number the song was, what tracks were before and after, the release year, the tone of the instruments—and why they chose to play with *that* particular guitar on *this* track, etc. What would have happened if they had played this song acoustically or with...never mind, I'm probably losing you. And there you have it, I almost hit a squirrel.

I arrived at Foxtail ten minutes before my shift and made the conscious decision that I would not let the impending doom of Calvin's visit stress me out. But I failed because I *was* stressed out. And this day wasn't going to get any better, no matter how well I planned to thwart the river of stress with a perfectly planned playlist.

Foxtail Coffee is an interesting place of employment. The branch I work at is actually called Foxtail Farmhouse because, somehow, we think by adding the word "Farmhouse" to the store gives it a hipster/rural appeal, like wearing a mesh trucker hat with skinny jeans. *Some fashion trends I will just never understand.* But my boss, Ahmed Patel, is a hard-working 40-something from Pakistani heritage who tries really hard to make this place work. And for the most part, it really does. The best thing about Ahmed is that he lets me play my playlist when I come into work. He knows that I am a true, albeit self-proclaimed, music expert, and it would probably be in his best interest to take whatever music knowledge I impart on him and accept it as gospel. That aside, the vibe is cool, and the employees and customers are really laid back. What we lack in steady customer flow, we more than make up for in authenticity. Our customers are true coffee snobs who really know the difference between iced coffee and a cold brew. Do *you* know the difference? If not, go Google it and come back when you do. Unfortunately, sometimes the air is so thick with attitude that it could suffocate you. And most of the time, I am the cause of such pomposity, but today that was the last thing I needed.

The morning kinda flew by with the rush of folks getting caffeinated-up for their commute. But then around ten, the line started to slow and reality set back in. Why was I so worked up about Calvin's visit? Why did I care that he actually *wanted* to spend time with me? I'll tell you why—thanks for asking, because every time that asswipe has spent more than 30 minutes in my presence, he has made me feel like one of the 10 worst human beings on the planet. And I don't even know how he does it; it's like a freakin' super power, I swear.

Oh, you haven't been to church lately, Nathan?

Oh, you have gay friends, Nathan?

Oh, you eat peanut butter straight from the jar, Nathan?

SHUT UP, CALVIN! I think I may have actually said that last

part out loud because my co-worker, Jessica, shot a very concerned expression at me.

"You okay, Nathan? You seem more quiet than usual, which I didn't think was humanly possible," she said—with much less sarcasm than you might think.

"Yeah, I'm ok. Have I ever told you about my brother Calvin?"

"Is he the asshole or the Jesus freak?"

I realized he was both, but she was probably trying to make a distinction between my siblings. I try to portray them accurately in conversation, but maybe I'm a bit harsh sometimes when retelling my tales of brotherly love.

"He's the holy one. But anyway, he kinda invited himself over for dinner tomorrow and it's stressing me out. I have no idea why, aside from the fact that he's probably going to find a new reason for why I'm inevitably descending to hell while eating dessert. Just hanging out with my family makes me a little uptight. Except my sister, she's kinda cool. But I guess I'm just worried he's gonna say something stupid or insulting or just generally rude in front of Frank and Claire."

"Nah, they're pretty laid back compared to you." Jessica tried to reassure me while not actually calling me out for being a hypersensitive prick. "I'm sure whatever he says will just roll off them. I mean, Claire just went to your house for Thanksgiving last week, you said. If she can put up with your family on a holiday, she's a keeper."

"I'm not dating Claire! Nor am I ever going to date Claire!" This was getting to be an exhausting conversation. Not the Claire part, that was kinda funny, even if it was annoying. No, the whole talking to Jessica thing. I needed to end this in a hot minute before she drained me of any possible good karma I might have left for the day.

"You're right, I'm sure it'll be fine," I said, hopefully, making her feel like she'd eased my anxiety. I needed the quickest verbal exit to this madness. You see, this is why I don't like many people—they talk too much. Or maybe, they don't like me because I insult them. Either way it's a win-win.

I finished my shift and headed home, thinking about what was to come and trying desperately to convince myself that tomorrow would be fine, everyone would get along great, and things would go smoothly—all this worrying would have been for nothing.

Ha. The worrying was the least of my concerns.

Chapter 3

the tuesday outing

Monday night was kind of a blur, as Frank and I devoured two bottles of chardonnay and all four sides of The Clash's classic LP *London Calling*. I often forget what a fantastic record this is from side one, track one, the title track "London Calling," to side four, final track, "Train In Vain," it is such perfection. I also love the fact that none of this is lost on Frank either. From the outside, Frank does not look at all like someone who would be this clever about music. He stands about 5'6 and is equally as wide. He spends as much time listening to classic alternative as he does weight lifting. Both are his obsessions, and he excels at both. With his crewcut and Freddie Mercury mustache, I hear he is quite popular among the fellas. He's been with Gary for three years now, though, so that was all in his past, as I met him only a few months before they started dating.

Frank piped up, "I don't know what I love more, Mick Jones' voice or Paul Simonon's bass playing. They both make me swoon."

And just like that, I remember that underneath all that muscle and hair is just a big girl wanting to get out.

"I'll go with Simonon's bass. His sound and swagger get me every time. Hey, what are you planning to cook for dinner tomorrow night? And by the way, in case I forgot to say it already, thank you for volunteering to cook, you know I suck at it, and Claire's not much better."

"I heard that!" Claire bellowed from her bedroom. "I can cook just fine. I can't help it if the two of you don't appreciate good quality Spam sandwiches or Ravioli."

She's right, if you can nuke it or fry it in a pan, Claire's got you covered. Which is actually more than I can say for my cooking skills. I swear to God if I burn one more Tupperware bowl trying to microwave Mac and Cheese, I'm gonna lose my stinking mind. But for tomorrow night I wanted something a little more "extravagant," so I opted for Frank's culinary skills. Not trying to make him sound like he is the stereotypical gay man, but he *is* the stereotypical gay man. Clean, neat, a good cook, and a little on the flamboyant side. But again, that's why I love him, he's extremely confident in who he is. And tomorrow I want him to be confident so that he can make a killer homemade vegetarian lasagna. Frank is also a strict vegetarian and keeps Claire and I from living on chicken nuggets and Oreos.

"It's no big deal" Frank said, laughing as he got up and started towards the kitchen. "I think I have everything I need, and, hopefully, this dinner will let you relax. You've been a real pain in the ass for the past couple of days, and I'm about done with you, mister. I should be the one stressing from what you've told me about him. He knows I'm gay and has told you multiple times that he has serious issues with it. Yet, he will grace me with his presence and even eat my very gay lasagna. I will assure him that he won't catch any STDs from eating it."

The next day was normal as we all went about our business. Frank went to the gym and came back with a couple bottles of wine and garlic bread to go with his pasta and salad. Claire had taken the day off, probably to distract me, but she said she had stuff to get done around town. I cleaned the house and still managed to drive over to the record store; since as it was Tuesday, there were new releases on the shelf. I was disappointed to find out there was nothing to add to the collection today, so I just perused the aisles until I was sure there were no hidden bootlegs or rare releases Rick was trying to hide from me.

Calvin arrived at 4:30 sharp. Claire greeted him at the door as Frank was still working on his masterpiece in the kitchen.

"Hey, man," I said, strolling in. "Good to see you. Thanks for finally coming over to our humble abode."

"Good evening, Nathan," Calvin replied.

And there it was. The low pastoral tone with a hint of judgment. It was going to be one of those nights. *And this is why I've stressed for the past five days.* Can you see it now, people? Nothing like getting off to a bad start from the first three words.

"Good evening, Calvin," I replied, openly mocking his tone. "I hope what we provide for you tonight will meet your presumptuous standards."

"Don't patronize me, Nathan. You know I come with no ill will to you or your friends. I am here to partake of some fine food and great conversation. If anything else comes of it, only the better."

What he means by "if anything else comes of it" is that if he can possibly convert one of us, or heaven forbid "save" Frank from the doom of his lifestyle choice, it will have been a good meal. He disgusts me in more ways than I can say. I mean, Graham is an ass, but at least he wears it on his sleeve. He'll tell you he's an ass, and he'll hold nothing back. Calvin is a sneaky ass. He'll pretend like he's talking kindly to you, all the while he's covertly trying to Jesusify you.

As if on cue, Frank walks in carrying some appetizers and almost drops his tray. This is so unlike him, as he is way more coordinated than I am, although that's like saying a panther is a little more graceful than a drunk and blind orangutan. I suspect it's because he could sense the tension that Calvin was throwing. He was already uncomfortable, and dinner hadn't even been served. The look Calvin gave him only added insult to injury. He glared, and then his eyes instantly shot down, like Frank was a leper not to be seen or touched. I imagined myself punching Calvin in his stupid face.

"Calvin, this is my roommate Frank. Frank this is Calvin." I introduced them as if they needed to hear each other's names. They both knew the enemy was in the room and they were doing their best to try and maintain some semblance of polite conduct.

"Yes, nice to meet you," Calvin answered, and even tried to sound pleasant.

Frank dropped off the tray of snacks and retreated back to the kitchen to continue with dinner prep. I was going to chastise Calvin, but I didn't want to draw more attention to the situation, so I let it lie. And I wasn't going to give him the benefit of having the space to say something insulting to my friend.

The angel that is Claire saved the day by making conversation. "Calvin, where exactly is your church? I've never been there, but Nathan always says it's not far from here."

"No, it's really not. Just head down Princeton Street to Mills and take a right; it's three blocks on your left. Small building with a small parsonage in the back. Quaint. Perfect for a single guy."

"Have you always been single?" Claire asked playfully. "No one on the horizon for the old Calvinator?"

Calvin was kind of taken aback by this question. *I guess he forgot how direct Claire could be.* It's a blessing and a curse of hers. Pisses lots of people off, but you never wonder where she stands on a subject. My family had long since stopped asking Calvin about his domestic situation, as he was married to his church, as he liked to say. He wasn't a bad-looking guy, just kind of bland and nondescript. I know that may be weird to some of you to hear me talk about my brother that way, but I can admit it—Graham basically got all the looks in our family. Calvin and I are pretty boring, and Marcie always had the cute thing going on, but, like Claire, battled her weight. I don't know if I've mentioned that before. Claire is not obese but is definitely a little on the soft side. She has used every diet trick in the book and still looks about the exact same way as she did when I met her in college.

"Well, if I have to answer honestly," he said in a whisper, as if his love life were some well-protected secret, "I stay single so that my focus and energy can be used in God's service. I don't have the time or the energy to court at the moment, but maybe someday."

Well, that's a relief. Calvin isn't going to let his flock of about 200 senior citizens go astray by possibly taking a young lass out to dinner. I mean, what would they do? Who would have the donuts ready for the 8:30 Sunday morning mass if he was out until 9:30 the night before "courting." *Who even says that anymore? Courting. What the frick, Calvin? Stop embarrassing me.*

"Well, dinner is served," said Frank as he brought out the amazing smelling lasagna. He really knew how to entertain. I mean, the place settings were perfect; he had some music playing in the background (a little Everything But the Girl from *The Stars Shine Bright* album: a thinking-man's Sade), and three courses laid out for us. A gorgeous citrus salad, his signature lasagna, and an apple crisp (which he knew was my favorite, so I can eat my stress away) waiting on the bar from the kitchen.

"Smells delicious," muttered Calvin, as if it almost pained him to give Frank a compliment. What. A. Jerk.

As we sat down, Calvin insisted that he bless the food, probably because he feared that a sinful gay pagan made it and if he consumed it, who knows how his eternal destination might be affected? I swallowed my pride and let him finish while stealing sideways glances at Claire and Frank. I'm not sure, but they almost looked as if they were about to nod off if he went on much longer. I forgot how long-winded Calvin can be with blessings. Maybe his congregation isn't really that old, maybe they have all just prematurely aged while listening to him droll on.

"So, I have got to ask you, Calvin—what do you think about Mom and Dad going away for the holidays? I was totally blown away by that! I mean, Dad never wants to travel at that time of year."

"Yeah, I was caught off guard as much as you were, but I am looking forward to being at Marcie's for Christmas. She and Joe never get to host a holiday, and I think it will be a really great time seeing the kids in their own place at Christmas."

I never thought of Calvin as sentimental, but this is as close as he'll get, so I guess I'll take it. The rest of the dinner conversation was fine enough, as was the rest of the night as we moved to the living room for drinks and/or coffee, as Calvin would never partake of "fermented fruit of the vine," but there was certainly forced dialogue between he and Frank. I don't know why Frank volunteered to do this. He is so uncomfortable right now. Maybe there is more prejudice out there than I realize, and this is why he and Gary keep their relationship so private.

"So Frank, will you be joining us for Christmas?" Calvin asked, hoping for a negative response.

"Yes, both Gary and I have been invited by Marcie, so I am really looking forward to it. It is going to be really special this year," he added, sounding almost giddy.

"Oh, *Gary?* I assume that's your "special friend," Calvin said in his best pastor voice.

"Special Friend" what the fuck, Calvin? *What are you, eighty?*

"Yes, Gary and I have been partners for a few years now," Frank responded, as if the wind was taken out of his sails.

"Well, I should get going," said Calvin.

Not a moment too soon. *Actually, about four hours and a lasagna too late.* I don't think I hid my excitement at all.

"Yeah, tomorrow's going to come early," I said almost tripping over myself to get his jacket. "Thanks for stopping by. It was great to catch up a bit," I lied, without throwing up in my mouth.

"Well, I really appreciate you all having me. We'll have to do it again. Thanks again for cooking, Frank," Calvin was saying as I partially closed the door on him.

Do it again? *Like hell.* I'd rather pan fry my underwear and eat it like a pizza before putting up with that again.

After closing the door, I could see the expression on Frank's face, and it was not what I was expecting at all. He was ready to explode with laughter. *What was this? Hadn't he just gone through the same torture I did? How could this put anyone in a jovial mood?*

"What is that look for?" I asked a little curious and slightly annoyed that he wasn't sharing in my personal pain.

"Oh my God. I've been holding it in all night! I guess I have known your brother longer than I have known you, Nathan!" Frank said before guzzling both his *and my* glass of wine.

"What are you talking about?" asked Claire. "You haven't set foot in a church since you were ten. You told me yourself."

"Oh no, sweetie, I never stepped in *his* church, but he is a frequent flyer in *mine*, if you catch my drift."

"What!?" I stammered, putting the pieces of what he was insinuating together too slowly. I'm not the sharpest knife, but I think he's saying that Calvin has tried to preach in Frank's gay bars, right?

"He tried to preach at some of your clubs?" I asked like an idiot.

"No, dumbass," said Claire with a snicker. "He's saying your brother is gay!"

"Are you kidding, you think Calvin is gay?"

"Oh, honey, your brother is not just gay, he is Queeny McRainbow. No, really, that was his stage name for drag nights. He was a well-known regular at all the locations for years. Back when the Parliament House was jumping, to Firestone, to Pulse before the shooting happened. That's kind of when he dropped out of the scene. He told us his name was Craig Jones. And he was *very* popular. Used to have a line out the door of his dressing room after his performances, if you know what I mean. I have no idea how he has kept it so quiet and a secret from his churchy folks, but that boy is a legend in the drag circle."

Ah hell. This was going to change everything.

Chapter 4

gripping reality

So, what was I supposed to do with *this* news? I had a monumental, proverbial "bomb" dropped on me last night. Calvin, my self-righteous bother, who has always imparted his passive-aggressive judgement on my whole family, has been living a private life of drag show performances and *who knows* what else? This was more than I was ready to handle. I mean, I'd been dreading the whole evening for reasons I thought were familiar, but when the dust settled, I was left with this! Damn.

Frank, Claire and I ended up talking until well after 2 a.m. Frank let me into a side of his (and Calvin's) life that I actually knew very little about. Frank and Gary spent time with us, but I had never been to his clubs or hung out in his scene. Not that I am opposed to it, it just has never come up. So tonight, Frank told us of how he first met Calvin (or Craig, as he knew him) and how he would perform a cappella versions of 80's movie songs (usually from John Hughes' movies) while dressed in spandex pants and Jennifer Beals classic off-the-shoulder shirt look from Flash Dance. That image is now burned into my brain and I will never be able to escape it. You have no idea what it's like seeing your brother (who would not make a very pretty woman) in drag—even if it's just in your imagination. Or maybe you do. If so, then hat's off to you. But it wasn't sitting well with me.

I was in shock, upset, and depressed all at the same time. I mean, *how dare he?* How dare he have this secret life that he has never told anyone about. How dare my world get shattered like this. I can NEVER look at him the same way again. I am disappointed in his secrecy. Not with his lifestyle choices; he knows I have absolutely no issues with that. I am upset that he sits on a "throne" passing judgment while living two entirely different lives and has kept his whole family in the dark. *What am I supposed to do with this information?* Can I tell Marcie? Graham? I *for sure* cannot tell our parents. It was an absolute mess and I was having none of it. I polished off more wine than I should have, laughed, screamed, and probably even cried a little with my friends before I passed out on the living room sofa. Like Scarlett O'Hara, I decided to deal with it tomorrow.

Well, tomorrow came and I did not deal with it much better. I called in sick to work, as I was in desperate need of a mental health day. The next thing I did was put some music together. This is a must in most life-crisis situations. Not only can I lose myself in the selection process, but I may gain a golden nugget of wisdom from a song. They are the best sources of information and inspiration, so why not start at the top? I've already told you about my passion for Morrissey and The Smiths, and if anyone can take even more of a crap on your bad day, it's Stephen Patrick Morrissey. The Oscar Wilde of the music world: funny and sad and extremely honest all at the same time. Should this be a playlist or go straight to the jugular with Strangeways, Here We Come? Released in 1987, it was The Smiths "swan song" and one of their most personal and passionate records. As I listened to Morrissey lament on "Last Night I Dreamt Somebody Loved Me" the words in the second verse about losing hope and false alarms hit home.

I somehow forgot, in the midst of my anger and disturbance over Calvin's news, how this must be hitting him. He knows that I know now because he knows that Frank knows. He has been hiding all of this and probably living a pretty sad and lonely life. Instead of getting mad at him, I needed to surround him with acceptance and maybe even be the one to help him break it to the rest of the family. Thank you, Morrissey! See, I told you if you look to music for guidance in life, it will never let you down—ever. That's how music has always been for me.

All this thinking had both exhausted me and made me hungry. I had walked all the way from our house to my favorite record shop but needed some nourishment first. Across the street was the White Wolf Cafe, which was part hipster eatery and part antique store. Not as weird as you might think. I had worked there about a hundred years ago as a server and, even though I have moved on to greener pastures at Foxtail (my "career bar" is pretty low—don't judge me) I still enjoyed their Black Bean Hummus. So, I grabbed a table and perused the New York Times music section on my iPad while I tried to calm myself down and do some carb overloading. Their coffee was not top notch, but their atmosphere and food made up for it.

"Can I get you anything else?" The overly attentive and perky waitress said, jolting me out of the article I was reading, so startled I almost wet myself and lodged some hummus in my left nostril. *Great, I'm going to choke on a pita chip and die before I have a chance to reconcile my guilt to Calvin.*

"No, I'm good," I barely vocalized, sounding like a prepubescent middle schooler searching for his new voice. I paid and quickly headed across the street to the record store before I was taken out by bean dip.

"Nathan!" bellowed Rick, the grisly owner of Rock 'n Roll Heaven. Rick and I have a love/hate relationship. He loves me and I hate him. Every time I come in, he stands way too close and talks my ear off. Not that what he is saying is interesting at all, because it's not, but he is also, I don't know, just a little creepy. He is the type of guy who gives us dignified record collectors a bad name.

"What's up, Rick? Anything new since I saw you last?" I asked not really wanting him to reply.

"Well, you know Frank Turner is at The Social this Saturday, right?"

No shit, Rick, anyone who is anyone knows he is at The Social on Saturday, what do I look like? Do I look like I buy my music at Target, Rick? Do I? Again, that is what I want to say, but my brain spews out, "Yeah, that should be a great show. You going?"

Again, I don't really care, but I tend to get caught in these Venus-Flytrap-conversations with people. How do other people do it? How do they have meaningless conversations? I don't get it. Is it possible to contract muteness? I need to look into that.

"Yeah, I was given a few VIP lounge passes that I can't use—you want 'em?" he asked.

So this is how karma works, huh? Here I am wishing I could wrap Rick's head in duct tape and now he offers me VIP passes to the Frank Turner show. In case you're not familiar with Mr. Turner, he is one of the best singer-songwriters to come out of England in the past decade. Yeah, way better than that freakin' Ed Sheeran dude. Sure, Sheeran's pretty good—okay fine, he's really good, but Turner is much more my style. And Claire absolutely loves him. Ah hell, but if I take the passes, it's like I'll owe Rick. He'll never leave me alone. I'll feel forever in his debt. I'll feel like I really have to go out of my way to be nice and friendly and maybe even get him a Christmas card or something. No. I can't. No matter how much this will disappoint Claire and how much I will regret it on Sunday, I can't. I can't. I can't.

"Sure, I'd love them, are you kidding?" I reply. Is it possible that your brain and your mouth are controlled by two separate entities that live in your body? I mean, not even a millisecond ago there was no way on God's Green Earth I was going to take those tickets. And now, here I am. In lifelong debt to Rick.

"Yeah, here take them. You get balcony seating and some kind of food spread before the show. They are for industry folks, so, you know, press people will be there reviewing the show. Have fun! There's five tickets in there, so take your roomies."

"Wow, Rick," I muster with as much sincerity as possible, "that's really generous of you. We really appreciate it. Now how about ordering me that Queen Is Dead 5-LP Box Set?"

"Sure! I'd thought you'd never ask. I'll order it this afternoon and you should have it by next week. Let's see, that's $85 plus tax," he cheerfully announced.

Someday, there will be a Scrooge and Marley moment between Rick and I, when I come back to haunt him for ripping me off.

You see, I already bought that box set from Amazon for $65 when Rick screwed me out of the order last time. But I never told him that. I just acted disappointed when he let my copy go to some UCF sorority bimbo. (I'm assuming it was a sorority bimbo; I have no actual knowledge of that, nor do I think sorority girls are bimbos, just this particular one who bought my record, because why else would you sell my copy, RICK? It *had* to be for a hot girl; otherwise, you just suck.) So, out of guilt, and somehow hoping to start chipping away at the cosmic debt I'm now in with Rick, I make another purchase. I could have probably bought anything, but that would have seemed patronizing. This way it feels legit. Maybe I can get half of my money back on eBay.

I leave the record store in an even weirder mood than I did when I arrived, and then I get a text from Graham.

Graham: Hey, I just had lunch with Calvin, and I really need to talk to you. Free tomorrow?

Me (trying to sound cool over text): Yeah, how 'bout 12:30? Location?

Graham: Chili's near me? I have a doctor appointment in the morning. Cool?

Me: Sounds good.

Oh snap! Calvin must be freaking out and told Graham before I did! *What a dick.* Does he think I'm going to run over and say, "Hey, Graham, Calvin's gay. Not just gay but gayer than gay. Drag-queeny gay." No, I'm not that kind of guy, Calvin, sheesh. *Well, this will make for an interesting lunch tomorrow.* I'm not really surprised he told Graham already, though. Calvin and Graham have always been closer. They're only two years apart, and they always seem like they have more in common with each other than I do with either of them. There are three years between me and Calvin and another two years between me and Marcie. My parents were some busy folks, if I stop and think about it, which I try not to.

Well, this has been an interesting 24 hours. Hopefully, after I can commiserate with Graham, I'll feel a little more normal about it and he can help me formulate a plan for how we're going to move forward with this. *I can't even imagine telling Mom and Dad.*

Chapter 5

stop me if you've heard this one before

So, I worked the breakfast shift at Foxtail to make up for calling in yesterday. I needed the cash, and my Friday shifts could sometimes be a little light. I know that I really need to work on furthering my career, but at this point in my life nothing is really exciting me. If you asked my father, he would tell you that your career doesn't have to define you, it just needs to give you a paycheck. Unfortunately, that's not how I'm wired. I need to be fully immersed in my work, and it needs to inspire me. And, so far, "listening to music for money and having an arrogant view of it" hasn't turned up on any job search sites.

But Graham, on the other hand, epitomizes my father's work ethic. Graham and he are cut from the same cloth. Work, work, work, and reap the financial rewards. Don't have to really give a crap about what you're doing, just keep doing it and shut up. Sometimes I really wish I could be more like them. Actually, more often than I like to admit to myself. I find that, although I really love my life, sometimes I stress out about not really having a grip on this whole "adult" thing. I figure I'm going to turn forty someday and maybe I'll have it figured out by then. *Maybe?*

Anyway, I drive across town to the Chili's closer to where Graham lives. I do like this part of town, even though some of the folks are pretty pretentious. They have a right to be, I guess. They work hard to afford their luxurious lifestyles and I shouldn't look down on them too much. I'm not sure why he chose Chili's as he's usually much more "high-brow" than that. Nothing against the Chili's chain, but Graham usually requires valet parking. Also, he never takes a day off to go to the doctor, so I wonder what's up with that? Probably looking into a face-lift.

I arrive first at the restaurant and get us a table in the bar area, so I can take advantage of the free chips and salsa. I can't always guarantee that Graham will pick up the tab, so a poor barista's gotta do what he's gotta do. Also, I'm glad I'm here first because I kind of want to burst his bubble about knowing about Calvin. I figure it this way, Calvin came out to Graham yesterday and he figures he can have the "I knew first" moment. (I did that in air quotes with a wink, in case you were keeping up.) That would somewhat diminish that fact that it was Frank and his eyewitness observations of Cal's performances that were revealed to me first. So, my plan is to make a second or two of small talk and then-wham! Hit him with "So, Calvin's gay, huh? What do you think about that?" Yeah, I'll watch him look all puzzled, and he'll wonder how his little, lost, non-real-job-holding brother got the big scoop. I could almost feel my adrenaline rushing. I better stop before I pass out from the excitement.

I see Graham walk in and he gives me a wave. *Man, he looks like crap, good thing he saw somebody about that today. Probably hungover.* Wouldn't be the first time I saw him after a few days of binging. But that was usually tied to a beach getaway with one of his mannequin princesses.

"Hey, man, how's it going," he mustered.

Definitely been drinking.

"Good. We don't get to get out much together—what's the occasion?" I replied, holding back my excitement.

"Well, just some stuff I need to talk to you about."

"Yeah, I know, Calvin's gay, huh? Pretty crazy to come out after all these years. I mean, who would have thought— *Calvin?* The preachy one, right? Always telling Dad to go to church. Always having an attitude about everything. Yeah, man, I was as surprised as you are. I figured you and I would have to get together and figure out how to tell Mom and Dad. Good plan. Good plan."

"What *the fuck* are you talking about?" Graham asked.

He was actually looking like he was serious. Too funny.

"Get off it, dude. I know about Calvin. No biggie, Frank told me his back story, which you might not even have the details about yet, but boy—"

"Nathan, shut up. I have absolutely no idea what you're talking about! What are you trying to say? Calvin hasn't said anything to me about whatever it is you're claiming? Are you being serious, or is this some type of dumbass hipster conversation that never makes any sense to me? What in the name of all that is holy are you talking about?"

Okay, this wasn't going at all as I had planned. My bomb dropping was supposed to be working in my favor and elicit the kind of response that made me look cool to Graham. And, uh, the exact opposite was happening. I'm looking more like that awkward eighties-movie character who says really inappropriate things that make everyone uncomfortable. Except I'm the only one feeling uncomfortable. And I'm the one who said it, so I should not be both characters in this scene.

"So, you're telling me that you did not call me to lunch to discuss Calvin and his sexual preferences?" At this exact moment our waiter walks up to the table and probably wishes he hadn't. Nothing worse than two men discussing another man's sexual habits. He takes our drink orders (which should have been way stronger than a diet cola) and slinks away, probably never to be seen again.

"Again, I have no idea what you're talking about, but we'll get to that later. Holy crap! My brain *cannot* handle this right now. Damn it Nathan! No, I actually needed to talk to you about something. Is that okay, or are you going to continue this barrage of nonsense?"

He was getting really bothered, and now I not only felt awkward but kind of bad. I feel like I may have really upset him. Not that I ever thought Graham owned any emotion besides sarcasm, but that's not the point at the moment. I really hit a sore spot. It was time to back up a little.

"Hey, sorry, man—yeah, we can totally talk about that later, what's up?" I tried to remain focused so that I would actually pay attention to what he was about to tell me because I have developed a slight Pavlov's Dog reflex when it comes to my eldest brother. He talks and I stop listening. It has worked out remarkably well for family get togethers, but I'm thinking that this may not be the time and place for that.

"Dude," he starts, "I have to tell you something and please don't interrupt me because I won't be able to get it out if you do. A couple of months ago I started not feeling too good. Loss of energy, really bad issues with going to the bathroom, and I was losing weight. Well, I thought I was just dealing with some stomach flu stuff after visiting Venezuela recently. But it kept going. I finally went to see my doc and he sent me for some tests. Well, come to find out, I have stage-4 pancreatic cancer. Sucks, right?" His eyes were starting to fill up, and honestly, so were mine. "Anyways, I have about six months and they don't think there is anything they can do. I have been round and round, but I didn't want to say anything. But now I'm going to do some experimental treatments to try and at least slow it down, maybe extend my time, but it's not hopeful. The crap thing is I'm going to start losing my hair, so I couldn't put off saying anything. I'll be bald by Christmas and that would be a bummer of a time to bring it up. Mom and Dad don't know yet and they are going to be pissed that I waited until after they left to tell them. But I don't want to stop them from taking this vacation. There's nothing that staying here can help. Sorry to drop this on you, bro, but there's no easy way to say it."

What the hell is going on in my life? I can't even process this. Less than a week ago, my life was perfectly fine. A little unconventional, but perfectly fine. I had two brothers who drove me crazy, and now they are *both* heading down different trajectories in life than I ever could have fathomed even just a week ago. I wasn't sure if I was going to vomit, cry, or get up and walk out. I decided that none of those options were in the best interest of the situation, so I calmly took a breath.

"I don't even know what to say. Dude, I am so sorry. Is there nothing…where do we even go from here? Does Marcie know? Crap, Graham!" It was the best I could come up with in the moment. Not exactly Dalai-Lama-level comforting, but my brain wasn't firing right.

"No, I haven't told her yet. I don't want to stress her out. And you know how she's been the past year—always on the verge of a nervous breakdown it seems. I can't hide it from her for much longer, but I was actually hoping that you could break it to her for me? I know she's going to lose it, and I don't think I have the energy to handle that at the moment. Could you do that for me? I'd really really appreciate it."

Graham was right. Marcie was going to lose her shit when she found out. Not only is she one panic-attack away from Nutsville, but she is the kind of girl who doesn't do well with bad news. Not that anybody would do well with news like this, but Marcie is just on a different level. She will go to a dark place, and I'm not sure Joe will even be able to help her.

"Yeah, no problem. I will totally tell her," I said, knowing full well that I would be recruiting Claire to do the heavy lifting of that conversation.

So, we sat there for a while making small talk, ordering light lunches since neither of us could really think about eating, and generally being absorbed in the moment. I didn't want to talk, but I also didn't want to leave. I felt, probably for the first time in my life, like I just wanted to be around Graham. Like this time was more precious than I realized.

"So, what the heck were you trying to tell me about Calvin?" Graham finally asked. I was kind of hoping that his brain would not catch up to that part of our conversation.

"Well, he came over for dinner the other night and it was very interesting." I told him about Frank's run-ins with Calvin/Craig and how our brother had been leading a really different life than we thought. I had considered not going into so much detail since he was having enough issues in his life, but I had already opened the door, and quite honestly, I'm not a good liar. It's probably one of my only endearing traits, but I am really honest. Most of the time people wish I wasn't, but I probably don't like those people anyway. So, we conversed about Calvin, and decided that Graham would keep it on the downlow until I had a chance to talk to him myself. Which, having just been given this news by Graham, I felt compelled to befriend Calvin rather than humiliate him. *What was going on with me?* I have some of the most potentially humiliating news of all time, ready to rub it in his face, after all his years of condemnations, and I just wanted to make sure he was okay. Man, sometimes I hate maturing.

Chapter 6

losing my grip

I gave Graham a long hug as we exited Chili's and promised to call him soon. This was a complete transformation from the brother I had known for my thirty years on this planet. I have heard about folks finding God, or reinventing themselves, but I had never truly witnessed it. Maybe the next time I saw Graham he would be back to his old insulting me, womanizing self, but I was scared that was not the reality of the situation. I realize he left Janine not *because* of her, but *for* her. He was not going to bring someone else down this path with him. He never let any girl he dated get close enough to take care of him, and he certainly wasn't going to start now. I spent most of the rest of Thursday in a stupor. I couldn't believe what I'd found out about Calvin on Tuesday, and now *this* with Graham. I needed some air and some space. And some privacy. I decided that a walk around Lake Ivanhoe was in store, and a playlist, must have a playlist (this had to be thinking music, something instrumental-probably Irish folk, yeah that sounds about right). I knew there were not many people there this time of day and with the cooler November, soon to be December, weather, it was the perfect Florida walking season.

I walked for about two hours trying to piece together a semblance of what my world was looking like now. I have a brother who, whether he meant to or not, has been outed in his hidden lifestyle choices. Now, I have to convince him of two things. First, he has no reason to hide this from me. And second, he really should let the rest of his family in on it. There is more acceptance here than he realizes, and it would make his life a little easier to have some support going on. And now, my oldest brother is looking at the end of his life coming right at him. I need to find the strength to be his support and somehow be there for Marcie and my parents. I find myself in very unfamiliar territory. You see, I have always skated by in life, where my family is concerned anyways, as the brother/child who really doesn't have to do much. I mean, I'm not the oldest, so that burden has been lifted from me and with Graham being such a financial stud and Calvin taking on the high moral career, I was pretty much free to coast on irresponsibility. I mean, that plays right into my sweet spot. I'm also not the youngest or the only girl, which, thank the lord, both jobs fell to Marcie. She could be the baby of the family and get spoiled rotten, and as the only married one with children, she has an even more special role in the parentals' universe. And I am good with my role. Not too many expectations. And when I do anything worthwhile, it's like I won the lottery. *Oh Nathan, you have a bank account! What a good boy! We're so proud of you!* Really low bar for me.

Now, it's looking like I have to be the one to handle things. Ah, crap. I definitely need backup. Claire will know how to help. I have no idea how she does it because she's an only child with no one to look up to at all. Pretty uninvolved parents as well, and yet she always knows what to say and how to act. Yes. I'll ask Claire.

Well, that whole decision took me two hours to come up with. Like I've said, I usually spend the first portion of any major situation in full panic mode, and then slowly find my way back to normalcy, then somehow come up with a plan that basically still shoulders most of the job onto someone else. I'm quite the stud muffin of responsibility. *At least I have a plan.*

Claire arrived home and could instantly tell something was wrong. I'm not sure if she just wanted to avoid it or what, but she made a beeline for her room and I swear it felt like it took her forty-five minutes to change her shoes. Probably only five minutes, but I'm still kind of in shock here, people, so work with me. Finally, she entered in the living room, eyeing me suspiciously.

"What's wrong with you?" she asked in not the warmest Claire voice in the world, but it would do.

"Well, I had lunch with my brother, Graham, today." I tried not to sound emotional. And by her reaction, I had succeeded.

"Ah, how was Captain Dickpants?"

"Well, not as Dickpantsian as usual. He's dying."

"Dying of what? Boredom?" She was maintaining this conversation while checking her Instagram feed. I can't really blame her, though. I have been very outspoken regarding my overall annoyance with my siblings. In most cases, this would have been a perfectly normal exchange.

"No, he's really dying, Claire. Cancer. Stage four. Got about six months. I'm really freaking out over here."

And with that, the Claire that so many of my friends have come to rely on over the years, appeared in my living room. Her eyes softened and she was completely engaged in our talk. I needed that. I needed to know that she was invested because there was no way I was going to be able to handle this alone. I was going to need to be surrounded by a support team if I was going to be of any help to my family.

"Are you kidding, Nathan? That's awful. How long has he known? Why didn't he say anything at Thanksgiving? Is there anything that can be done?"

She was just trying to help, but all these thoughts had already swam around in my noggin all afternoon and I didn't really want to regurgitate it again out loud. I sat silently for a moment, and I think Claire could read my thoughts.

"It's ok" she said. "You don't have to talk about it. I'm just shocked, that's all."

"Thanks," was all I could muster. I didn't know my next step but admitting this crazy-ass day out loud to someone made it both more real and more acceptable.

"I am going to need a favor from you. I need someone to go with me next week. I have to break the news to Marcie.

Graham can't handle her potential breakdown right now, and I'm not sure I can either. I figure if you're there at least someone with some sense will be available if she decides to jump in front of a bus."

"Nathan, that's not funny. Don't talk like that if you don't want things like that to happen."

I'm not sure why people (not just Claire at this particular moment) need to tell me things like this. I'm not joking. I actually think my sister has the very real capacity to jump in front of a bus. Also, what is the thought process that actually saying something will cause it to happen? It goes right along with the misguided notion that hoping for something not to happen will prevent it from happening. Life just happens, people; we can't do anything about that sometimes. And I don't want to be alone when Marcie takes the great greyhound lunge.

I re-told the tale to Frank as he came home and we all decided that drinks were needed. I also broke the news to them that I had VIP tickets to the Frank Turner concert tomorrow night. As they were both super excited and Frank instantly called and invited Gary, we began to make our way over to The Mill for their delicious pizza and homemade Amber Brew. It was exactly what I needed after the day I had. These friends were my lifeline, and I was soon to find out, more needed than ever.

Chapter 7

showtime

Frank was leaving for Portland on Sunday, so he spent most of the day Saturday packing and hanging out with Gary while I worked. He was going to shoot pictures for the opening of a new museum based on the history of still photography, which, ironically, seems a little redundant, but that's why I'm a barista and he's the artist. He and Gary made sure that he brought enough warm clothes for the Pacific Northwest. Gary stands as quite the contrast to Frank. At least 6'3 and rail thin, he and Frank sometimes remind me more of Laurel and Hardy than a romantic couple. I'm not sure what Claire did, but sometimes I envy her nine-to-five schedule.

Jessica was already at work when I arrived, and the place was really bustling for a Saturday. There was a line to the door, and she was the only one behind the counter. I forget how much business jumps when the weather dips even a little. A lesson for those uninformed about Orlando weather. We only have two seasons here: not so hot, which runs from November to March, and really freaking hot, which is the rest of the year.

"Thank goodness you're here," Jess said as I started making the drink she had laid out.

"Sorry about this. I would have come in earlier if I'd known you'd be so swamped." I lied. I was exhausted from not getting much sleep last night, but I did feel bad she was so in the weeds.

"Where's Ahmed or Bert?" I asked her. Bert was our other co-worker who was an extremely caffeinated individual and a fanatical theater and movie buff. We get along because of our obsessive interests, but he is exhausting to work with sometimes.

"Bert will be here in a few," Jessica replied, never missing a beat on taking her orders. Well, we could use the help, so that'll be welcome.

The shift flew by with Jessica, Bert and I laughing and making more beverages in a day than I have seen since I've worked there. The temperature was about sixty degrees outside, which is a beautiful Florida day, but you would have thought, if you saw our customers, that it was Ontario in December, as opposed to Orlando. The conversation was pleasant enough and just the break I needed from my family drama. When four o'clock hit and it was time for me to clock-out, I wanted to hug both of them for giving me "peace of mind," but that would have seemed out of left field and maybe a bit weird.

I drove home listening to my Frank Turner playlist in prep for the show. I had gone online and downloaded his current set list and made a playlist of those exact songs. It's a good thing that I have these passes and that my peeps are going with me, because it's like I'm living the concert before the concert, and that is the exact sort of reason that I talk myself out of going out. "Well, I've already heard the show today," I'll say to my brain. "Why don't we just stay home and watch something artsy on Netflix?" and somehow that usually wins out. I'm not sure how my brain can be so on-the-money with trivial musical history and so incredibly stupid and easily duped.

The four of us arrived at The Social thirty minutes before showtime, which drove my roommates crazy. As big of music buffs as the three of us are, only I care about watching the roadies perform endless soundchecks to get everything just right. Turner didn't have an opening band tonight, so it was just him and his backing band, The Sleeping Souls.

"Check out this spread!" Gary exclaimed, not sounding cool at all. The room was not as big as I had imagined, and there were only three other people there: local music reviewers, I'm guessing. They did a great job of keeping to themselves and not imposing any conversation on us as we made our way down the shrimp and deli selections.

"Frank told me about your brothers—not a great week for you, Natie," Gary said while loading his plate with shrimp cocktail. He was not the strict vegetarian that Frank was, so he was in heaven. Also, his calling me Natie is one of his endearing qualities that only slightly drives me nuts. But I don't say anything because, well, I'm just not that confrontational.

"Yeah, I'm still processing it, but I'm feeling much better today. I'm actually thinking of inviting Calvin out Christmas shopping next week and maybe talking to him about it."

"Let's do it!" Claire butts in, sounding way too excited. "Frank and I want to get a jumpstart on it after he gets back on Tuesday, so let's plan on all four of us going on Wednesday. Maybe you could talk to him before then, and if he's cool with it, we can start to make him feel a little more comfortable with it before you blow his cover at Christmas. I'm assuming that was your plan. It's a pretty Smythe-type thing to do. Drop news like that right smack dab in the middle of Christmas dinner. Classic Nathan."

"I would never do anything like that," I said, realizing it was the second time I had blatantly lied that day. Before yesterday, I don't think there was any doubt in my mind that I would have totally hung his news out there in front of the turkey and everybody. But now I know that there will be a more somber feel to this holiday with Graham's newly minted diagnosis. I don't think that would be the day to "out" my brother.

"I want him to know that I know and that I want him to stop lying to me and be more open. But as far as when he tells Marcie and my parents, it's his business. I kind of already blew it with Graham by giving him the news, but his head is so far out there, he's not really concerned with Calvin's life choices. At least he's got a life to make choices in." I know that came out harsh, but I also know that my brother would say the exact same thing and not hold it against me for saying it either. He's pissed that he's sick and he's gonna go down fighting, but he knows he's gonna go down.

Turner and the band kicked off the set with his anti-Trump song 1933 from his new album, *Be More Kind*. The rest of the set was a mix of old and new stuff and was absolutely perfect. We had a great view, great sound, great food, and great company. I couldn't think of a much better way to end one of the worst weeks of my life. Thank God for music.

Chapter 8

bringing the peace

I decided to take Claire's advice, so on Monday, after work, I drove over to Calvin's parsonage and hoped to find him home. I was nervous as hell because I had no idea how he was going to react. This was foreign territory for us. I was used to him always being the one to "pass judgment," and now I'm sure he felt that I was going to be *that* guy. *Here's hoping I'm not.*

I knocked on his door and could hear him moving about; finally, he showed up.

"What do you want, Nathan?" he asked in a gruff tone I have never heard from Calvin. *This may be more difficult than I thought.*

"I thought maybe we could talk?"

"About what? I have nothing to talk to you about."

"Well, your attitude says something different. Why are you

doing this, Calvin? I know that you know Frank. And I know now that you've been hiding your personal life from all of us. I also know that I don't give a shit. I'm a little pissed that for all these years you've been passing judgment on others when you've been living the exact same life of "sin." I'm not sure how long you thought you could keep this a secret. Or why you've kept it one, but you're my brother and I love you, no matter what type of idiot you're being. So, stop being a jerk and talk to me, talk to all of us, and come clean. This is a new time and world, Calvin, you have to see that. Society is way more accepting of any lifestyle. Ok, I'm babbling, say something, would you?"

Calvin looked down and stayed quiet. I could see he wanted to talk but piecing the words together was going to be a challenge. He was also going to make sure that it was perfect. He did not want to misspeak. I knew my brother well enough to know that much.

"I have lived this way for years. Since my early twenties at least. I had my first partner in college, and I knew that this was going to be an issue for me. I was pursuing a career of faith and this lifestyle, in most circles, is very taboo. So the lies started. And the hiding started. And then it just became a bigger and bigger web of lies that became easier to manage as two separate lives. I just assumed a totally different persona when I was out in the clubs or with a new partner, which I could never really have, because of my other world. The other night was the first time that my two worlds have ever collided. I've skated the line for a long time, but I knew it was eventually going to come out. When I first started going out, I wasn't the only one in hiding. There were so many of us. Guys and gals who have made their way in the world under the guise of being straight. Just never talking about their personal lives. Things are different now, though. You're right, the world has changed, but in many ways it hasn't. My congregation is old, and they will leave me. I will never serve here again if this comes to light. But what the other night showed me is that I need to be truthful. I need to make this public on *my terms* and not someone else's. If I were caught, like I was with Frank, and it wasn't at my brother's place, it could turn very ugly for me as I would not be able to direct that narrative. I'm hoping you will let me. I'm hoping that you and I can come to some agreement and you will let me play this out the way I want to."

I was equally amazed at both his bravery and fear. My brother had always come across as one of the most vanilla, boring, and unemotional guys you'd ever meet. But, here was some passion. Maybe this was his true self. Finally, able to combine both of his worlds. Not having to hide anymore in front of me. I don't know what came over him, but I certainly wasn't going to be the ass he suspected me of potentially being. I have earned his suspicion, but I wasn't going to let that play out today.

"Thank you. *Thank you* for being honest. So, let's just start fresh and figure out how we proceed from here. You and I are good. This is fine. I just really want you to be happy, and if that means you still need to lead these two lives than so be it. But I don't want you to live it in front of Graham and I anymore."

"What do you mean *'Graham and I'?* He has no idea about any of this."

And with that, any lightbulbs that were off in his head suddenly became illuminated. I imagined Calvin punching me in the face. I think if he were actually able to castrate me with laser beams from his eyeballs he would have at that moment.

"Fuck, Nathan! You fucking told him didn't you! *Really?* Do you have any idea what he's going through right now. Fuck! Fuck! Fuck!"

Those were more fuck's than I have ever heard Calvin utter in his entire life. All in a row, too. Pretty impressive. But it was time for my damage control instinct to kick in. I have a lot of adulting to grasp in the next few months if I am ever going to navigate the minefields I will inevitably encounter with my family as all this is going on. *Holy crap, talking is exhausting sometimes.*

"Yes, I know what he's got going on. I was having lunch with him when I kinda let it slip. I knew he met with you the other day and I really thought you had told him. I'm so sorry, but to be honest, I don't think Graham gives any more of a shit than I do. He's so preoccupied right now, I'm sure it's cool. That's really the least of your concerns. You need to tell me what we're doing with the rest of the family. Are you telling Marcie? Or Mom and Dad? And can I come in? I'm tired of talking to you through your screen door."

Calvin looked like he was calming down a little as he let me in to his living room. His place was small and really neat, but for the first time I noticed how few things he actually owned. Was this because this life was not his true self and he needed to keep up appearances in case a parishioner came over?

"Well, I think I need to tell Marcie first and then I'm actually going to open up to my church. It may be the end of the road for me here, but I can't live like this anymore."

"What about Mom and Dad?" I asked, "I know Graham kept his cancer a secret so as not to ruin their trip. Do you want to do the same thing?" I already knew the answer. There is no way he wanted to do this over the phone to our parents. This was going to rock their world and he needed to have them face to face. Mom was going to be a wreck and Dad will never be able to hide his disappointment. I felt really bad for Calvin as I imagined him having to tell them. Maybe I could offer my moral support and be there for him.

"Mom and Dad already know. They've known for years. I told them after my first experience in college because I needed to always have an honest relationship with Mom. Dad really didn't care either way, but Mom has been nothing but supportive. She just feels bad that I feel like I have to hide it." Calvin said, like it was no big deal.

What family is this!? How do I know so little about these people that supposedly raised me? *What the hell?* Maybe I wasn't switched at birth, but they were switched on me while I was away at school. Mom was supportive? *What!?* Dad doesn't care? *Holy what!?* I don't get it. I mean, I'm happy for him, but completely lost right now.

"So let me get this straight, you're pissed that Graham knows, but you're okay telling Mom?" This was straight out of *The Twilight Zone*.

"Yeah, Mom's pretty cool. But you know Graham. I mean, before this cancer thing anyways. He's really different now. You should really talk to him, oh wait-you already DID!"

Sarcasm was not Calvin's strong suit, he should really leave that to the experts like me, but this time he pulled it off pretty good. Maybe there was hope for him after all.

"Okay" I said, "but we can't hit Marcie with a double whammy about both you and Graham, and she needs to know about him before we get to Christmas. He says he may be losing his hair by then, so she needs to have a little warning. Can we wait for your big announcement until after then?"

"No, I really need this to be out there in my church by the holiday as well. If they are going to push me out, I want them to feel a little guilty about giving it to me for a Christmas present." Calvin was almost smiling when he said this.

I'm starting to wonder if he is hoping that he is fired. I'm beginning to think that this is the push he has needed to get his life out in the open. And now, maybe he feels like there is no turning back. There is no doing this halfway. It's all out there or not.

"Okay, well, I was also here to invite you to go Christmas shopping with Claire, Frank, and me this Wednesday after Frank gets back from Portland. Maybe I could see if Marcie is available as well. You could tell her with a support group around you and we could both gently break the news to her about Graham."

Calvin looked both confused and touched. I have never witnessed either of my brothers crying (except for the time

Graham accidently hit Calvin in the mouth winding up for a slapshot while playing street hockey...that was funny as shit), but now, within the same week, I feel like I'm about to have seen them both weeping. Calvin stopped just short of that (thank God) and agreed to join us.

"I was afraid Frank wouldn't want to see me after realizing who I was and that he and I were already connected. I almost went out on a date with him one time, if I remember right. We just made out a little at the club, I think. Wow, that was back in the Parliament days...good times."

You know, I'm really okay with both of their sexual choices, but the thought of Frank and Calvin swapping spit was probably as close to as completely repulsed as I could be. I know that sounds homophobic, maybe, but I would have preferred not getting those details. If it was a choice between watching my parents honeymoon sex tape (please tell me that does not exist) or witnessing Frank and Cal, I don't really know where I would land on that.

"Okay, well, now that that's out there, let's remember he's taken and that you kissing my friend is gross. Dude, I'm just getting used to the fact that you're gay. Not sure I'm ready for details yet. Thanks, though."

"Sorry, Nathan," Calvin was smiling. My discomfort was obviously amusing him, so at least my feelings were good for something.

I got up, gave him a bro hug and told him we'd meet him at the mall on Wednesday. Now to get Marcie on board and hope for the best.

Chapter 9
re-meet the parents

My parents FaceTime'd me on Tuesday from Denver. We have always vacationed in Colorado, so I wasn't surprised to find them there. It is beyond so beautiful there, and the people are so laid back. Someday I will find myself living there or in the Pacific Northwest, I'm sure. I mean isn't that where everyone goes if you want to become a professional barista? I'm not sure that's a thing, but if it is, I'm so there.

I was going through all the options I had worked out as to what I was going to tell my parents. Do I tell them I know about Calvin? Do I break the news gently to them about Graham? I decided that the potential to screw this up was high, and my rate of screwing things up was astronomically higher than most humans, so the best plan for me was to just shut up. That I am good at.

"So, how's your trip going?" I asked, jealous of the snow I was seeing behind them.

"Oh, it's amazing, Nathan!" Mom was beaming. She and my dad are an amazing couple. They can actually go for years never being apart and still be totally in love with each other. I mean, I get sick of being with myself for too long, never mind somebody else. I don't know if I will ever find love like that in another person. An album collection, yes, a human being, not so much.

"That's great. Where are you guys off to next? Do you think you'll be spending a lot of time in Denver?"

"Well, that's one of the reasons we're calling you. We are thinking about buying a piece of property out here. We don't know if we want to sell the house in Florida or not, but we definitely want to live half the year out here. What do you think?"

"I think that's awesome, Mom. You'd give me a reason to head out there every year and you guys really should enjoy yourselves."

"Good. Don't tell your brothers yet, we are just in the "thinking-about-it" phase. I don't want to get anyone all upset."

What was this new thought process my family seemed to have all of a sudden...*Since when was I the best guy to keep secrets?* I actually suck at them, or at least I did as a kid (my parents couldn't ever tell me what they were getting my siblings for Christmas because I was guaranteed to blab). But maybe I seemed like a responsible soul all of a sudden. Or maybe they knew I was such an extreme introvert that the potential of me actually striking up a conversation with someone was pretty low compared to my mostly extroverted family.

Mom also probably thought that I was going to freak out the most. I'm pretty OCD and really hate change, so the thought of my parents moving should have struck a nerve of panic in me, but I'm so much more mature now (that's sarcasm, by the way). But I am happy for my parents, especially because of everything else that's going on. We may all need a place to escape to now and then, and if there is anything I know about my folks, it's that they will always make sure there is room for all of us there.

I ended the conversation with my parents feeling really good about them and where they were heading in life. Between that and the thought of Christmas shopping tomorrow (I'm still a little kid when it comes to the holidays), it was time to put my Christmas playlist together.

Now here's the thing about me and Christmas music. There are some non-Christmas albums that will always remind me of the holidays—probably because I bought them around that time, such as The Smiths *Louder Than Bombs*, any album by The Tragically Hip, any Harry Potter Soundtrack (I'm serious), and Barenaked Ladies classic album *Gordon*. But there are also Christmas albums that go on the list as well. You have to have Sting's *If On a Winter's Night*, *A Punk Rock Christmas*, and the 1987 great *A Very Special Christmas* (which I originally purchased for Sting's Gabriel's Message, but ended up liking the U2 and Pretenders tracks even more). Also, the classic Michael Buble, and believe it or not, Garth Brooks—both have incredible Christmas albums. Throw in some Bing Crosby and Aaron Neville and you have a well-rounded Christmas set of tunes. Now, most folks have their own favorites and holiday music can be very personal to most people. The problem with most people is that they have really, really bad taste in music, so that's why I'm here to help them. They shouldn't waste their time listening to sub-par Christmas ditties, when right here, on my iPhone, is a perfect playlist. I'm always happy to share my opinions and song lists with people, which, I can tell, always makes people really happy. It's obvious in the way they are always in a hurry to end the conversation so that they can get home and download the tunes. I'm like a musical elf. Santa's little musical helper. You're welcome, Christmastime! Now let's get shopping! Oh, yeah…there's that whole bad news thing. Why couldn't they both have broken out their news in August? I mean, that's a month that needs a little help—hot as hell and no holidays to look forward to. It's like the opening band of the calendar world, dragging out the wait just to get to the good stuff. But that's not how this is going to play out. I need to sprinkle some Christmas magic into this turd pie of news.

Chapter 10

it's time

the tale was told

We arrived at The Florida Mall (my least favorite mall in Orlando, but closest to Marcie) at around 10:30. I wanted to be there at ten, for no other reason than I thought I needed to get the maximum amount of Christmas shopping done today. Frank, Claire, Calvin and I arrived in my Civic and waited for Marcie outside of the Apple store. Marcie was dropping her kids off at daycare and meeting us. Marcie was a stay-at-home mom, who didn't stay at home with her kids. She put them into daycare as soon as she could and spent her days meticulously cleaning her home and trying to launch some sort of online business. There had been more than a few that might as well have all been named Pyramid Schemes 'R Us. She also watches a lot of movies and is always trying some new diet and/or recipe on Joe and the boys. She is really happy, but I'm not sure exactly where she is going in life. She's kind of a wanderer. But then again, I'm a thirty-year-old barista.

Marcie came bounding over to us really excited for the day. I don't think many people call her to hang out, so you could tell she was really looking forward to this. She also inherited Mom's gene of wanting all her siblings to get along and hang out. I mean, I want to get along with all of them, I just don't need to see them to do it. It's probably better if I don't see them very often, actually, to maintain an even better relationship.

"So, who are we buying for first? Mom? Dad? Graham? Me?" She laughed but was serious about wanting a plan.

"Well, Frank is picking out something for Gary here at the Apple store, and I'm buying my parents an iPad so that we can finally FaceTime like your folks do, so should we start here?" Claire said.

"Heck yeah!" Marcie was just glowing. It broke my heart a little, knowing that Calvin and I were going to totally destroy whatever Christmas goodness she ate for breakfast that had put her in this fantastic mood. I quickly went from being Santa's elf to The Grinch. And not the cute, animated one voiced by Benedict Cumberbatch, but the gross Jim Carrey one.

Once Frank and Claire had made their purchases at the Apple store, we wandered around aimlessly. While I always loved the idea of going to the mall and finding that perfect something for someone at the holidays, it never quite worked out like that for me. There just seems to be more and more useless crap every year, and I just end up finding something really unique at a mom-and-pop shop in Winter Park or ordering something they really want off of Amazon. Frank, Claire, and Calvin were spending most of the day together and I had a feeling this was really good for Calvin. He was laughing and looking more relaxed than I have seen him in a while.

Marcie and I walked together ahead of them. The initially excessive energy seemed to be waning, and she was actually in a pretty quiet mood.

"Whatcha' thinking about?" I asked her.

"Oh, just a million different things, really. You know, how is the holiday going to go? Hoping Mom and Dad are doing well. Little stuff," she replied, seeming distracted.

I had absolutely no idea how I was going to bring the subject of Graham up to her. She didn't seem like she could focus on anything. But there was never going to be a good time, and I had promised him I would take care of it. I can't have the first chore that he gives me on his long path of illness be a complete failure. I needed to get Marcie alone, and I needed to get her sitting down. As if on cue, Claire calls up to us, "Hey guy, we're stopping in here for a bit." And all three of them jetted into The Art of Shaving store.

"That's cool, we'll wait for you out here," I said, walking Marcie over to the sitting area outside of Starbucks.

"Isn't this enemy territory?" She smiled at her own lame coffee joke.

"I think we are safe," I said with an exaggerated eye roll.

"I actually really need to talk to you, and I'm afraid that it's serious."

"Oh, Nathan, are you okay? What's the matter, hon?"

"Well, actually it's not me. It's Graham."

"He doesn't have an STD does he? I knew he was going to get one from one of those sleezebags he's always hooking up with. He's sick, isn't he?"

"Well," I said, not really sure how to answer. *Why does she go from zero to one hundred instantly? And why is she trying to figure out what I'm going to say before I say it? God, that's so annoying. Shut up and let me talk, Marcie. This is going to suck bad enough already*

"No, he doesn't have an STD; it's actually much worse than that. He has stage four pancreatic cancer. His outlook's not good. But he wanted you to know before the holiday as he's probably going to really look like shit then. He also wanted me to tell you because he didn't think he could handle telling you. You're probably going to cry, and he is too exhausted to deal with that right now, I guess. He knew that Calvin and I would probably keep it together and that was easier for him," I said, knowing full well that I almost cried like Tammy Faye Baker right in the middle of Chili's.

Marcie wasn't taking it well. Not. At. All. I was on the brink of being in the middle of a full-blown nervous-breakdown shitstorm if I didn't get her to pull it together and quick. She was shaking and starting to cry, no not just crying, but that sobbing you do when you can't even complete a sentence and there's snot coming out of your nose and you're actually drooling. Yeah, that was on the way. *What the hell was I thinking? Why was I trying to handle this alone?* I mean, I'm about as capable of handling emotional wrecks as I am at handling Rick from the record store. I'm an idiot when people are in distress. My first instinct was to take my jacket off and put it over her head so I could hide her from making a scene, but that didn't seem like the next best step. I decided to try talking her down.

"I know, this really sucks, huh?" I quickly said, hoping to stop her hemorrhaging emotions.

"It sucks!? It sucks?! That's the best you can say, right now? It way more than sucks, Nathan! Your brother is dying!"

That worked well. Good lord, if that was my best shot at calming her down, what the hell was going to come out of my mouth next? I almost couldn't take the thinking, so I just spoke whatever came into my mind, hoping for better results.

"I know he is, Marcie, and do you think this is easy for *me*? Do you think that I have enjoyed knowing that I was going to have to break this to you today? Do you think I like being the bearer of this news? Well, in case you were wondering, I don't. I hate it. I hate that he's sick. I hate that you didn't know, and I hate that I even have to say it out loud! But, you know what!? I bet Graham hates having cancer more than I hate any of this!"

She just kind of sat there and stared at me. Did that actually work? Did I actually form a cohesive enough stream of thoughts together that she might calm the hell down? Take that, stupid left frontal lobe! I guess my brain and mouth *can* function together if given the right mixture of panic and crisis.

"I'm sorry, Nathan. I shouldn't have yelled at you. I'm sorry. What are we going to do? How bad is he?"

I could tell she was trying her best and this was when I needed to turn the old, "Let's watch Nathan take care of his siblings" show on.

"I don't know. I don't really have any of those answers yet. I just know right now, I'm giving Graham space and checking on him from time to time and being there to support him when I can. I don't think he is looking for anything from us other than to just make him feel as normal as possible at Christmas. You obviously need to bring Joe up to speed so he doesn't say anything stupid."

"Yeah, that'll be a small miracle," she said, although I'm not sure why. I made the comment about Joe more as a joke. I didn't actually think he would say anything stupid. Joe was a pretty calm guy. I thought he would be cool. I don't get why my sister is mean to Joe sometimes. She's pretty neurotic. I'd say he's a keeper if he puts up with her.

Calvin, Claire, and Frank walked up and could see that Marcie was a bit of a wreck. Claire bent down and hugged her, causing Marcie to begin bawling again. *Thanks for that, Claire.* I'm sure on some level that is a sweet gesture, but right now—not what I needed. I gave Calvin the "I handled this one; your news is all on you, bro" look. And while I'm not sure he got it word for word, he took Marcie by the hand and led her to another table in the back of the Starbucks dining section. At this point, I figured we owed the Seattle coffee Goliath a good sum of our money, so I went to the counter and ordered 5 Gingerbread Latte's. *Why?* Because when you're suffering from some type of drama the first thing you need to do is suck pure sugar and caffeine with a dollop of whip cream through a straw. So, "Yes, those will be Venti."

As I got back to our table, I could see Marcie and Calvin sitting still in the back, then Marcie was laughing and hugging Calvin. *What the hell?* I deliver news that, by the way, isn't even *my* news, and I get yelled at! Calvin has his own personal drama to sell her and he gets a hug? *Ugh, the burden of being the chosen one.*

"Your brother is adjusting to his new life quite well, I think," says Frank with a hint of a "proud parent."

"I think he's going to be fine," adds Claire.

Well, aren't the two of them precious? Of course he's going to be okay. He's handling his transition to a new "normal" with my two kick-ass roommates! Yes, I know that happens to be them, but if it wasn't for my ninja-like social skills, this whole "is Calvin able to function in a society like a real boy?" thing wouldn't be happening. That's right, the bearer of bad news for my sister and the maker of new friends for my brother. I'm a freaking rock star.

"I'm glad we were here for you, Nathan, you'd have been lost without us," Claire boasts.

"So lost," Franks adds.

They don't get my genius.

Chapter 11

holiday preparations

I contacted Graham a couple of days after we all went shopping and let him know that Marcie was up to speed. He said that she had called him, and while she had mostly kept it together on the phone, he was concerned she was also in denial. He was starting his experimental treatment next week and still had a couple of weeks before the holiday to get in as much time at the clinic as possible. I asked if he needed me to drive him back and forth, but he told me that he had hired a personal assistant, Anne, who was going to work with him through the whole process.

"Are you seriously trying to get a fling in while you're full on battling the cancer demon?" I laughed, partially joking. It would be *so Graham* to do something like that.

"No," he said in a more serious tone than I had expected. "She's not my type, and I really couldn't be bothered with that at this point. Between the puking, exhaustion, and intermittent pain, disappointing a chick in bed does not sound like a good time."

"Oh, so she's smart," I quipped. I was hoping that our old-time brotherly banter would keep his spirits up. "Then she's definitely not your type."

"Thanks, dillweed. Yeah, she's smart and cute and working on her doctorate in education, so yeah, not my type. She works as a personal assistant while putting herself through school. Basically, she's just a walking calendar and reminder system."

That's great, I thought to myself. I don't really care and didn't really ask expecting honesty. It sounds like he could do all this with Siri, but maybe he wants the human contact. As a passionate introvert, I don't really know what that means.

As we worked our way toward the holiday, I picked up more shifts and generally got myself into the Christmas spirit. I decorated every room in the house and listened to my Christmas playlist non-stop. I even added some new tunes this year. Barenaked Ladies holiday album is so great that I can't believe I forgot to include it! I made it my personal goal to try and sell as many people on this classic as possible. I'm pretty sure Ahmed from work bought one, or at least he told me he did. He could've just wanted me to stop playing it at work so often.

Frank and Claire are also both really into the holiday spirit, which makes it so much more fun to go through, as opposed to the humbugs I'm usually stuck with at work and at the record store. I talked to Mom and Dad again and they are moving forward with the purchase of a condo in the middle of Colorado somewhere. They're not sure if it will be in Denver or further west, closer to Aspen.

It was an overcast Wednesday when I was chilling at home contemplating what culinary delight I was going to make for dinner: chicken nuggets (still an all-time favorite of mine—and I can sneak them in when Frank the militant vegetarian isn't around) or pop in a pizza, when the doorbell rang. Kinda weird because no one ever visits us, so I assumed it was a wandering school kid trying to get me to either order more magazines I don't read or buy popcorn. I was hoping for the popcorn because that might become a course in my dinner tonight. But, to my dismay, it was Calvin. Not that it wasn't nice to see him, but I'm really stinking hungry and he can be chatty.

"Hey, man, come on in," I said as I opened the door, hoping for him to decline.

"Thanks, Nathan. I was hoping you were home. Are Frank and Claire here?"

"No, both are at work." Oh, sure, *now* you care about my friends. You've never cared about them in all the years we've lived together, but now that they are on Team Calvin, all is well. Man, sometimes I am one bitter dude. Not very St. Nick of me. *Gotta work on that.* Maybe I should get a personal assistant as well, if nothing else, to remind me to stop being an ass.

"Oh, well, I'll just ask you."

Thanks for the enthusiasm, Calvin.

"I was hoping the three of you could come to service this weekend as I'm going to finally reveal myself to my church. It could get really ugly and I would love to know that there are at least a couple of faces in the crowd that will have my back."

I couldn't think of anything that I would rather do less than to go to Calvin's church. Absolutely anything. I mean, I was trying to come up with something, anything at all, to say in the one point-five seconds I had time to think before my mouth spouted, "We'd absolutely love to come and support you. I wouldn't ever want you to go through that alone." Which was the exact polar opposite of what my brain wanted, but I knew that he really needed us, and if I know Claire, she would be so pissed at me for failing my brother. She really felt like this was a big deal for him and could not see herself to be annoyed by like I was. I shouldn't say annoyed, but I really feel like he could have dealt with this a long time ago and not burdened me with it now. You know, because it's all about how it's affecting *me*. So now, we'll go and sit in the middle of the Holy Blue Hair Assembly of Winter Park, hoping to escape with our lives as Pope Calvin declares he is really RuPaul in disguise. I'm telling you, that sounds like a good time.

"Thanks, man, I really appreciate it. I can't tell you how much it means to me to have you guys support me. I really thought I was going to be fighting a much more uphill battle, but so far, I feel really good about it. I know that as bad as it will be on Sunday, I will come out better for it on the other side." Calvin was again actually beaming, and I felt really good about the fact that I hadn't really done anything, yet I had dramatically improved my relationship with my brother. Usually, I put in no effort and don't get nearly the results, so, win for me!

Calvin stuck around, so pizza it was. I was not going to share the last of the nuggets, and this way I knew I wouldn't have leftovers. Smythe boys have always been able to tackle a whole pizza pie. Claire came home first and gave Calvin a big hug (before saying hi to me by the way) and re-enforced the bad decision to go to his church on Sunday. I already knew Frank would be a yes, as he seems to have a very personal vendetta against any organized religion that thinks a same-sex couple should not get married. I had to say I agreed with him there, but I was way less vocal about it. Nor did I see the need for leaving my house on a perfectly good Sunday morning to stand in support of that. I was way more on the sidelines of support.

The rest of the week seemed to fly by, and I found myself staring Sunday morning in the face. I knew this was going to be difficult for Calvin, obviously, but he didn't seem to realize that I had to go to a church where everybody knew everybody and I'd have to endure at least ten minutes of banter with an old lady who was going to sign me up for a support group she was sure I needed. Not that this has ever happened to me, but this was how the morning was playing out in my head as I laid in bed hoping to oversleep and miss the whole thing.

We arrived a whole five minutes before service was about to start to find Calvin standing at the back of his church deep, deep, deep in thought. I tapped him on his elbow and gave him a little wave. He nodded, barely acknowledging me and went back to his pre-game meditation.

We found a row about halfway down the church and I could actually feel the stares of the congregation as we sat down. Now, it didn't help that Frank wore his most flamboyant striped shirt and overly skinny jeans (which, I must say, do not compliment him) but I think they were more concerned that we were at least thirty years younger than anyone in the building and probably thought we were only here for the free coffee and donuts in the lobby.

The service began smoothly enough with some awful organ music and hymns that sounded both familiar and comforting for some reason. They also included a Christmas hymn which put me in a better mood as I thought about what Frank was going to cook for me to take to Marcie's house: butterscotch cookies, as I am allergic to chocolate. *I will definitely request those as soon as we leave here, so I don't forget. My* personal assistant, if I had one, would be taking my cookie order—maybe Graham will share his on weekends?

Finally, Calvin stood up to speak. He looked like a man on a mission. I don't know if this is his normal preacher face, but if it is, it is good. Like a cross between Tom Brady with two minutes left and Mother Teresa as she gives you crap about not sending in that money for those kids over there somewhere.

"My friends. I have some news to share with you all today," Calvin began. "This is not tied to any sermon series except maybe one I preached on last year about loving your neighbor. I have welcomed many of you into my house and into this church. Many of you have shared with me times of struggle, times of fear, and times of pain. But now, the tables are turned. It is my turn to share my pain, shame, and heart with you. As many of you know, I am a single man. I have always stated that I am married to this church and this congregation. Well, that is only partly true. While I do love all of you with all my heart and will always be here to take care of any and all spiritual needs you may have, there is a bigger reason why I am single. A reason that, until very recently, I had never even shared with my family. For I did not think that my family would accept who I am. But that all changed with the love of my brother, Nathan. He is sitting right there in the blue polo shirt."

Really, Calvin? All one hundred plus, cataract-blurred sets of eyes were on me. *Could this get any worse?*

He continued, "I finally told my brother and his friends my true reason for not having a spouse or children. And that reason is that I stand here before you, a proud gay man."

You could have heard a pin drop. Well, I could have, I don't think any of these old coots could've heard it. As a matter of fact, I was really praying that they heard Calvin. But it was eerily silent. He paused to let it sink in. And then it happened. A couple in the third row got up and walked out. They glared at me as they passed, and it was all I could do to refrain from flipping them off. Maybe I wasn't going to be on the sidelines for this one, because for the first time I was pissed for Calvin. Another couple got up and left. And then a third. But most stayed. Not saying much, but not moving either. And from my peripheral vision, I saw Frank stand up. What the hell was he doing? He started clapping. This was not some sort of LGBTQ rally, Frank; this was the College Park Lutheran Church 9:30 a.m. old people service—sit down! But then, like a bad eighties movie, another man stood up and clapped. And another. And another. Before long, I was the only person sitting in the whole church not clapping. Finally, when I realized what was happening, I got up and joined in. This was amazing! Calvin stood there with tears running down his face, not able to contain himself! His world, which he was so afraid of abandoning him, had just welcomed him with open arms. This world which he tried to hide his true self from for fear of banishment, was going to let him live. Let him be true to a truth that he didn't even know how to live in yet. Wow, almost like a Christmas miracle. *Well done, old people.*

Chapter 12

well, the weather inside is frightful

So, it's Christmas Eve and we are all getting ready to head over to Marcie's tomorrow. I actually feel good about this holiday. Marcie had told Joe, so he and the kids are all aware of Uncle Graham's new hairdo. I have also spoken with Graham and Calvin this week and they are both ready with Graham feeling as well as can be expected. Claire and Frank are going to join us, as is Gary, so it should be a nice day for all.

Claire, Frank, Gary, and I arrive at Marcie's at around eleven in the morning, and her kids are still going a little crazy over their gifts. Their oldest, Owen, is five and he is going absolutely nutso over his Harry Potter Lego set.

"Uncle Nate, come look at my wego's!" he exclaimed as I came through the door. He called me Nate, as does his mother, so I was okay with it. He had started to build what looked like the beginnings of Hogwarts, but I'm pretty sure he was using Ron's head as a doorknob.

Their younger boys, Nicholas and Timothy—three-years-old twins—were bouncing from toy to box to discarded wrapping paper with equal enjoyment in all three. Yes, she and Joe had three boys, who were all very bright, although Timothy was much further behind vocally than his brothers, but I'm sure they would all catch up in time.

Joe was in the kitchen tending to all things turkey because our family insisted on having the stuffed bird for both Thanksgiving and Christmas. I could see he was deep in thought, but I wanted to make sure I contributed my customary insincere offer to help, which I knew he would decline, before I slinked out the door for my first of many Christmas whiskeys.

"Joe, can I help with anything?" I said, already heading to the liquor cabinet.

"Yeah, sure," he replied. "Can you check on the potatoes in the oven, and if they're not done, I need you to start setting the table. If the potatoes *are* done, turn the oven to warm so they don't get cold."

Check to see if a potato was done? He would have been better off asking me to assist with child birth. *I have no idea if a potato is done, what do you do, ask it?* This is why I was heading for the booze, Joe. That's my usual job on Christmas. *Where the heck is my sister?* She handles these things, not me. See, Mom, this is what happens when you flaunt around the Colorado countryside. I end up helping birth a potato.

"How do you know if it's done?"

"Stick it with a fork," Joe directed.

Oh, that clears up everything. Stick it with a fork. I'm going to need more than that. "Ok, Joe, I've forked it. Should it be doing something special, cause it's not."

"No, if it goes in smooth like when you're eating it, it's done."

Okay, now there was some real direction. "No, they are definitely not done. As a matter of fact, your oven's not warm at all."

"Oh crap! Did Marcie not turn it on?"

I assumed that this was a rhetorical question because saying, "Not warm" definitely implied "not on." But I could tell by Joe's expression, and the sudden extreme panic in his eyes, that the assumption was not a good one.

"I can get them started for you—what temp do you want?"

"They are going to take over an hour!" Joe said this like it was common sense, which he should not assume, since I did not even know that sticking them with a fork provided magical insight to the potatoes' current condition. "Forget it! We'll just have to skip them this year."

He was obviously agitated. For my sister's sake, I was hoping she had contracted whooping cough overnight, as that was one of the only excuses he looked like he was going to accept.

At that moment Marcie wandered in, with not much of a sense of Christmas Dinner urgency, I might add, but more like a disinterested observer.

"Why didn't you turn the oven on, Marcie? There is no way we're going to have potatoes in time for dinner now.

Hope you like stuffing because you need to throw in an extra box of that."

Marcie didn't respond, just absentmindedly went to the pantry and searched for another box of stuffing. Now *this* I could handle. But what was going on with her? She looked like one of my stoner friends from college, but without the good mood.

"I can do that for ya, Marcie." I said, again hoping for a negative response while making my way to the door with my eyes on the prize bottle. I assumed they needed to talk because the Great Potato Disaster seemed like it was actually something deeper. She just put the box down and walked out of the kitchen, not talking or even looking at me. Maybe she was really not ready to see Graham today. Maybe this was a bad idea, and we should all just load up and bounce over to Cracker Barrel. I'm sure they are having a really good spread today. But that was not to be as Joe gave me the "look" and I took up the box of bready goodness and began the microwaving process.

As Joe and I finished dinner and setting the places (with lots of help from Claire-thank god!), I could hear that all of our guests, which really just meant Graham, were here. I could actually make out Marcie's voice and she sounded perfectly fine. I don't get women sometimes, which is probably why I am still single. Moody as all heck one minute, and then fine and laughing the next. That's way too many emotions in a really short timeframe for me.

The table was set, and Joe called for all to "Come and get it." The three kids sat off to the side on a makeshift table that was basically three tv trays set up together. They were happy, and basically had their own separate courses, so it was cool. Calvin said a much more abridged version of grace. (I like this new Calvin.) And we all began to feast. Graham barely ate, but he was keeping up his spirits as best he could. He did look like crap, I have to admit. He was getting thinner both in the belly and on his head.

"So, Graham," I said, "How's that new assistant working out for you? Is she actually keeping you on track or have you completely driven her nuts yet?"

"You know, I almost invited her over, but I knew you were going to be here, so I didn't really want you to ruin something good in my life." *Well, at least his sarcasm still worked.* "She's great," he continued, "really, really on top of things. She's also really funny and quite a good cook. She has me eating healthier than I ever have, although I keep reminding her that I want to go out eating whatever the hell I want, not salads and fruit trays. But you really should come meet her, Nathan. Or any of you guys, actually. I've told her about my whole family, but you all are avoiding me like the plague, which I don't have, by the way, and I'm beginning to think she thinks I'm just being delusional about even having a family. So, come over after the new year and meet her. She is going to be taking care of more and more stuff, so it would be good for her to know some faces."

That kind of brought the mood down, but it was all stuff that had to be said. We can't ignore the fact that Graham is dying, and I'm glad my folks weren't there to see him, but I didn't realize how hard this was going to be.

Calvin mentioned to us that he was not sure how long he was going to be staying at his church. His congregation had more than accepted him, but now that he was out and open, he wanted to make sure that he could bind in matrimony as many same-sex couples as possible. He wanted to make sure that the gay and lesbian community of Orlando had a church that welcomed them and was open to going out into the community and giving back. He felt that this was a good way of keeping to doors of accepted alternative lifestyles open. This was going to be great for Calvin as he needed to align both his spiritual life and his personal life, and this was the way he was going to make it happen.

Well, with that, Frank felt that this was as good a time as ever, I suppose.

"Calvin, we may be one of your first ceremonies," Frank said, his face a sight of pure joy. "Gary and I are getting married! He proposed last night, and I accepted."

Well, that took Claire and I both by surprise—not that I didn't think it would eventually happen. But Gary has been extremely private about his relationships in hiding everything from his family, so the thought of him going through a ceremony blew my mind. Knowing that he was going to share this with his family and how this might backfire on him struck me as pretty damn brave.

"You see," Gary started to explain, "after talking to Calvin this week, I realized that I couldn't continue living like this. I needed to be out and open with everyone in my life, not just my close circle. And seeing how you all rallied around Calvin, and knowing that you will all rally around Frank and me, that was enough for me to say that now is the time. I want to do it before I regret *not* doing it."

Wow, Graham was in pretty great spirits, and now Gary and Frank with this wonderful news, there was such a warm and glowing feeling. This was possibly going to be one of the happiest holidays I would remember.

"Well, isn't that all just fucking wonderful!" Marcie exclaimed. "Too bad my husband has been sleeping with his business partner for the past six months! Yeah, you heard it, Jill! And I'm leaving him. Effective immediately!"

And just like that, the Christmas happiness was destroyed. Marcie stood up, grabbed her keys, and stormed out of the house. I heard her car race out of the driveway and screech as she took the corner. Well, now this is uncomfortable. Here we sit with Joe and the kids, who are all crying at this point, staring at our plates full of way too much stuffing. Well, Christ, Marcie! Who is going to have the balls to break this silence!?

"I may be a gay minister, but that doesn't mean I won't come over there and punch you in the throat! Did you seriously cheat on my sister, you freaking dumb mother-nutter?" Calvin exclaimed, trying to keep his cursing kid-friendly, which was funny as hell.

With that, Joe hung his head and said nothing. He realized quite quickly that he was surrounded by his wife's family and this was not going to end well for him. He looked sheepishly at the floor while all three of his children were being attended to by Gary and Claire.

"It's true. I came clean to her last month after she started to suspect my long hours were more than just extra time on the clock. I don't even know what to say to you guys. I didn't know what to say to her either. I made a mistake and screwed up."

"Screwed up?" Now I was getting hot. "No, this isn't a *screw up*, Joe, you invited her whole family over last month, while this was still going on! What kind of psycho moron are you?"

As much as I wanted to continue down this road of berating him, I was also becoming more and more aware of my nephews and how this was already going to scar them well into adulthood. I needed to get this conversation over and figure out how to move on.

Claire was on my wavelength and took the kids with Frank and Gary and went to the back living room. This provided not only physical distance to our conversation but was visually far as well, as I was not sure if either of my brothers were going to beat the tar out of him or not. This was their baby sister he had just done this to.

Graham was the first to talk after the kids left.

"Joe, I'm not going to pummel the dead horse that has already been beaten here, but you have to know how stupid you look to your kids right now. I mean, maybe they don't get it, but they know Mommy's mad and Daddy did something really naughty. You have to clean this whole mess up at some point, but right now you need to make this house right. Those kids need you, and so help me God, if you bad mouth my sister to them, I will come back from the grave and kick your ass. We already had enough bad news to give my parents this week, so I guess we can wait a little to see how this pans out for you two. You're welcome."

"I don't expect anything from you guys. I know that I need to fix this, but I don't even know what that looks like right now."

"I can tell you what it looks like," I interjected. "It looks like you apologizing to my sister, somehow separating yourself from your business partner, and fixing your relationship with your kids."

Joe slouched in his chair and continued to stare at the floor. After what seemed like forever, Claire returned to the dining room.

"Well, I don't know about the rest of you, but while you are all verbally beating Joe up, which you deserve, you piece of crap, I called Marcie. I'm going to go meet her in a few, so you need to take the three of us home, Nathan."

"Where is she? Is she okay?" Joe's voice was quivering a little, but he looked rather unaffected by this. Possibly shock setting in.

"If you think I'm going to give you any info right now, you're out of your freaking mind! She is safe, but you are not getting anywhere near her at the moment. She needs space and you need to take care of your kids."

"She's my wife! I deserve to know where she is."

At that moment Joe suddenly realized he was surrounded by Marcie's three brothers and Frank and Gary who were not about to listen. I don't know if you remember, but Frank can be quite intimidating looking. The odds were definitely not in Joe's favor.

"Maybe you should just calm down a little," Frank suggested as he moved closer to Joe's chair.

Joe seemed to think this was a good idea, sat back down, and didn't bother Claire for more details.

Graham started coughing terribly and I realized that this was a strain that he was not ready to take on. The reality of how sick he is was becoming more and more evident. I forgot how much cancer sucks until I saw my big strong brother starting to shrink. I swear he looks like he's aged since he got here this morning. *Stupid Joe.*

We all left as soon as we felt that Joe could handle actually watching his kids and not lose his mind on them. It was not their fault that their dad was an asshole. But too often anger is misdirected at the weaker people in the vicinity.

Once we got in the car, Claire told us that Marcie was going to meet us back at our place, so she had a place to spend the night. She was hysterical and not sure what she should do next. Maybe Calvin's pastoral superpowers could be used for good at a time like this.

Chapter 13

post-christmas blues

Only so much beer was going to help Marcie calm down that night, and I think she did a great job surpassing that amount. She cried, yelled, cried some more, and eventually passed out on our couch. Gary spent the night with Frank, and Claire and I went to bed once we felt she was no longer a threat to herself or others. She was not dealing with this well, although I'm not sure anyone who finds out their spouse is sleeping with the person he/she is working with does, but I'm really worried about her. She was already panicked about Graham, and trying to process Calvin, and all the while she was keeping her own little secret. *What is with my family lately?* Every one of them is a big house of liars. The more I think about it, I am amazed and scared that I have somehow become the poster child of sanity. *Who saw that coming, right?*

My head was spinning, if I had to be quite honest with you. I have seen personal crisis strike each of my three siblings in the past month, and I was right smack dab in the middle of this storm. Death, divorce, and coming out, were some of the most challenging emotional obstacles that people are faced with in their lifetime, and here I was staring at all three in the face. There was no amount of record-buying therapy that was going to make this feel better. I was sure that I would be called upon in the next calendar year in ways that I have never thought I was strong enough to take on and I know that life will look a lot different this time next year. When people think, "Hey, we need a strong rock to lean on for this emotional crisis," Nathan Smythe is not the name that comes up, but yet, here I am.

As I adjusted to my new normal, I also faced the ugly truth that it was December 26th. This is one of my least favorite days of the year, for the mere fact that I am a Christmas season fanatic, give me Hallmark Christmas movies and some Bing Crosby and I am one happy dude. I really wish I could wake up on the 26th and all the decorations could be gone, and there would be no signs of Christmas left. As I said, I absolutely love the holiday, but when it's over I want to get back to reality as quickly as possible. Stop with the Christmas music for another year, and don't even think about making me drink any eggnog. But enough about my drama. *What was going to be my first step today?* I know we have to get some of this out to my parents, but that was a potential disaster I was not ready to handle.

Marcie woke up around eight and I was impressed by her

lack of a hangover. She seemed ready to take on the day while I was still battling my over-indulgence of stuffing.

"You want some breakfast?," I asked as she seemed to be getting her belongings together.

"No, I need to get going. I need to get the kids and try and figure this stuff out. I mean, do I move out, does he? Am I keeping the kids, is he? I know their schedule and what they are doing, but I really don't feel like spending any time there. What is the first step in the divorce process?"

"Are you sure that's what you want? I mean don't jump the gun just yet."

"Nathan, all I know is that if I see that bastard right now, I may find a new use for that cast-iron skillet you just bought me. I need some space. Lots of space, but I don't want to be away from my kids right now. I need them, so I need to make this work somehow without having my mug shot on the front page of the Orlando Sentinel."

We chatted some more, and I told her she was able to spend time here any time she needed to get away. She wanted to make sure that Calvin and Graham were okay with her, so she was going to call them later in the day. I decided I needed to see Graham as well, and since the idea of going out and seeing more Christmas décor all over town sounded absolutely awful, a trip to his house didn't sound so bad. He never decorated for the holidays. I wondered, as he was facing this terrible disease, if he was regretting little things like that. I hoped not.

I arrived at Graham's at eleven in the morning as I knew he said he was going for a short treatment first thing this morning. Kind of a crappy way to top off the holiday, but I'm sure he wasn't looking at it the same way I was. I walked into his living room and I heard him coughing in the back room.

"Graham—hey it's Nathan! You need anything?" I called down the hall.

And with that a short brunette walked out of the back room. She was definitely walking with a purpose, and I was suddenly a little scared.

"Who are you?" she demanded.

"Uhh, I'm Nathan, Graham's brother. I'm here to see him."

"Well, he is not going to be seeing anyone today, sorry. That treatment this morning was a doozy. I'll let him know you were here."

"No, I think I'll go up and see him, if it's all the same to you. I am his brother, you know."

"I'm sorry, I don't care if you are the Queen of England, you're not seeing him today. I'm paid to take care of his business, and today he is none of your business."

Who the hell was this woman? She stood barely over five feet tall and could probably command Patton's army. By the way, did I mention that she was absolutely stunning? I mean, it's been a few years since I went on a real date, but this woman was causing some uncomfortable feelings in my stomach (this was not the stuffing). She was completely captivating. I wanted to push back and say, "No damn it, I'm going up to see my brother, get out of the way, tiny woman!" But that is not at all what came out. It was a lot more like,

"Ok, well, have him call me when he's feeling up to it. We had a rough day yesterday and I just wanted to bring him up to speed on stuff."

"Oh, Marcie, right—is she going to be okay?"

Okay, well, she knew about Marcie, so Graham felt close enough to her to let her into the details of his life that happened just *yesterday*. I guess she can't be *too* bad. I'll let her stick around for a while. I told her about my night with Marcie and how I was hoping that she wasn't going to fall off the deep end and she listened intently. Like, really intently. Most of my family never really listens to me like that. As a matter of fact, there aren't too many folks on this planet that actually listen to me at all, never mind with intent. I found myself saying way more words than I needed just to make sure the conversation wasn't over too quickly, like I actually wanted to talk to her. This was another feeling I was not used to at all. I was the one who would stare at his cell phone when it rang wondering why anyone would use this thing to actually talk to other humans when you could just text.

"Well," she finally interjected, "I really need to get back and make sure he's okay. I'm definitely not a nurse, but I also want to make sure he's comfortable. Kinda what I'm getting paid for."

"Sure, sure-um, if you need any help at any point, I would be more than happy to stop by when I'm not working. I mean, Graham and I are tight (lying to her already—not a good start, you idiot!), so I'm sure he'd love to have me around. Can I give you my number in case you need it for anything?" *Damn I'm smooth.*

"Yeah, sure, why don't you leave it on that pad over there and if I need anything, I'll give you a ring. Cool? I've really got to go. Nice to meet you Nate."

"Ok, I will. Nice to meet you too, Anne." Nate? Really? Well, it's kind of cute coming from her, so maybe I'll deal. She went back to Graham's bedroom, which was kinda weird, but I guess he expects it now, and it certainly wouldn't be the first strange woman to go back there. I left my number with my name and the stupidest smiley face on the note, just like I was in eighth grade again. I don't think I could be any more positive that she is never going to call me. I will definitely have to make the first move.

But then she called me as I was driving home, which caught me a little off guard. I tried not to drive off the road and sound way cooler than I was. What the heck? Why am I like a nervous teeny bopper all of a sudden? *This is not normal.*

"Hey, Nate, it's Anne. I was hoping that maybe you could stop by tomorrow. Graham wants me to go through some of his stuff and I may need help getting it out of his attic."

"Yeah, no problem, what time? I can either come before or after work. I start at ten and get out at five."

"Sure, let's do it after you get out, since I don't get here until the afternoon. Thanks, see you tomorrow."

As I hung up, I felt like I was going to burst. I completely missed my exit and found myself ten miles down the road in Altamonte Springs. This was okay, since I was near the mall, I would stop by and soak in some of the remaining holiday spirit. I have never soaked in the remaining holiday spirit. Never. But I found myself smiling a lot and putting together a new playlist in my head. This one would not have any songs in a minor key, I don't believe. No, this one would be lots of sunshine, since now that Christmas is over it's time to get ready for spring, right? McCartney had a little ditty called Silly Love Songs—that's a good start. I mean, don't read into it or anything. I just met this girl for crying out loud. It's just a nice peppy song, so back off will ya?

Chapter 14

a sort of homecoming

The next day I arrived at work about fifteen minutes late, which I really need to work on. Behind the counter, Bert was working on organizing the mugs, and I remembered that it was just me and him on this shift until Ahmed came in at one. Could be a good thing, I thought, maybe frantic spazzy Bert will keep my mind off the family drama.

"Hey Bert," I called across the bar.

"You're late. Why can you never get here on time?" He sounded even more snarky than normal. *This was going to be an awesome day.*

"Yeah, sorry, man, lost track of time. I'm telling you it's going to be my New Year's resolution to get better at that." I lied.

He looked at me for a moment. I would tell you that I thought he was contemplating something deeply, but this was Bert. Smart guy, but not really deep usually.

"Well, thanks for being honest at least and not making up some BS excuse about traffic."

So, that was pretty much the vibe of the day. Bert and I conversed about the films he caught over the past few weeks which included some holiday classics like It's A Wonderful Life (he loves it), Elf (he hates it) and Christmas Vacation (which believe it or not, he actually likes) as well as some really obscure holiday films from Sweden and Germany that made Bert sound like a movie snob, which is exactly what he was going for. Bert is about my age (pushing thirty), super skinny, and constantly looks like he's sick. You know, bags under the eyes and not-so-great posture. He's a really great guy with a bad attitude. I mean, he'd give you the shirt off his back while bitching about it the whole time. But his demeanor and conversation, for which he is never lacking, kept my mind free from drifting into panic mode. When I did have a moment later in the day, though, I started to stress while thinking about meeting Anne that evening. I don't know exactly what she needed me for, and I've only been face-to-face with her for about ten minutes, but she definitely made an impression. Like I said, I haven't dated seriously for a couple of years—aside from some scattered group-dates here and there, but I was a little weak in the knees after leaving Graham's yesterday.

Let me bring you up to speed on my love life. It sucks. There, you are up to speed. I date women who I have very little in common with and get myself into emotional spiderwebs and have a tough time leaving. Then, once I have exhausted all chances of there being the slightest possibility we're compatible, I bail. Gasping for breath. I'm really much more of a solo guy—Captain Quirky and all, but I really do want to find a soulmate one day. I see my parents and I know it's possible to totally connect with someone. I want that. Now, I'm jumping the gun even imaging that Anne is that person, but I know that I think I might want to possibly, maybe, spend more time with her. But for now, we'll start with this afternoon.

I got to Graham's at about five-thirty and she was already trying to get up into the attic to retrieve some of his stuff. Graham was there sitting in a folding chair, looking very pensive.

"Hey, man," Graham said as I walked into the garage. "Anne's trying to find the Lost Ark up there, but I don't think she's having much luck."

"What exactly is she looking for and why do you need it so desperately right now?" I asked, watching her struggle trying to get down the ladder with what looked like a box from 1942. She looked really good, even when she was sweating. *Good lord, I'm a mess.*

"Dad gave me a box of his Red Sox baseball cards from the fifties and I want to make sure that I pass them on to Marcie's boys."

I still had no idea why he needed this to be done pronto, but I'm sure his thought process was all over the place right now, so I was just here to help. I grabbed the box from Anne and gave her my best "How you doin'?" look, which went completely unnoticed, but I was just laying groundwork. It wasn't the box he needed, so I told her I would take a look up there. We spent the next hour going through boxes full of crap—so many—until we finally landed on the jackpot. I convinced Graham to get rid of about half of his junk, and he promised to go through the others a little at a time. I know that he has no intention of doing that, so I made a mental note to throw away one box every time I stopped by to check on Anne—I mean, Graham.

Anne and I made pleasant enough conversation and I could tell that she truly appreciated the help, but this was not the time to ask her out for coffee. She was tired, it seemed both mentally and physically, and I needed to spend more time with her to try to figure her out.

"Can I help you with anything else before I go?" I asked, trying not to sound desperate.

"No, I think we've got it, but I'll give you a call if I need anything."

"Feel free to keep me on speed-dial," I said laughing.

She did not laugh. "Yeah, I still have your sticky note, thanks." she replied, which means she didn't add my number to her contacts immediately after she got off the phone with me last time. I could suggest that to her, but she probably has a handle on how to use her phone, so I won't go there.

I left Graham's and headed home. It had been a good day. Graham seemed in good spirits, and I got to spend more time with his personal assistant, who, I think I may be having feelings for. Not sure, but I think so.

My parents arrived home on January 6th, ten days after I last saw Graham and Anne. After a very quiet New Year's Eve, Calvin and I decided to meet them at their house. It would not take long before they wanted to see their kids, and there were a few things that they needed to know. Deep breaths, everyone.

Mom was really excited to see us, and they both looked like they were well-rested. They both enjoyed traveling, especially road trips, and this one, with the thought of a potential new dwelling, really seemed to have lifted their spirits. *Glad I was here to change all that.*

"Well, isn't this a nice welcome home! Two of my boys, here to greet their momma." Mom was always overly sappy when it came to us, something that has never been lost on me. I watched closely, as many of my friends came from broken homes. Mom may drive me crazy at times, but I always know I have a place with them and that she, and my dad, love us unconditionally.

We went through the normal pleasantries of asking how the rest of their trip was and mom broke out her iPad and showed us countless pics of mountains and snow and other things you never see in Florida. Finally, I could not take it anymore, so I needed to get to the reason why we were here.

"Well, while we really did miss you, we are here to give you guys some news that is not so great. We need you to know what's been going on."

The tension grew to nearly unbearable. I don't even know how a parent reacts to the bad news of a child, and what I was about to give them is some of the worst news possible.

I began with telling them the story of Calvin coming to dinner and how Frank was well aware of his other life that was going on. I gave my mom a little crap for being in the loop and not telling us, yet I really respected the fact that she was letting Calvin live his life, while keeping it completely quiet. Then I tried to brace myself.

"And there's something else you need to be aware of. Graham met with us recently and told us that he is really sick. He has been diagnosed with stage-four pancreatic cancer. He is trying to do some experimental treatments but it's not sounding good. He is losing some of his hair and some weight as well. So, he's not the Graham you left, but he wants you to know and he really didn't want to ruin your trip." *But I think I just ruined their lives.*

My mother was crying before I even finished telling her the whole story and Dad was no better. They had nothing to say at first and then my dad just started to lose it a little.

"Are you sure there is nothing else!? Why didn't he tell us sooner? Why did he wait so long? *I am NOT going to bury my child!*" And with that, he stood up and stormed out of the room. I know that he needs to let it out, but there was nothing that was going to change. And yeah, Dad, I'm sure he would have loved to find it earlier; I'm sure he's not happy about this either. But those are not things I will say to him now, or ever, as he is a man who needs to deal with tragedy in his own way. Mom continued to cry and finally Calvin got up and hugged her. I think that is really what she needed at the moment and I decided right there that I was not going to talk anymore. As it was, I don't know how I am even going to bring up Marcie. Well, I didn't have to wait very long because Calvin seemed to think this was the right time to bring up more bad news. *You are a pastor right, Calvin?*

"Mom, we also have some news about Marcie. She left Joe on Christmas. We don't know how this is going to go, but he was cheating on her."

My mom just started to shake and weep even more deeply and I was sure I was about to see her go into cardiac arrest right in front of me. Calvin continued to hold her as we brought my dad up to speed when he finally came back into the room.

"Well, Joe's one dumb sonofabitch if he thinks he's going to do better than Marcie. He better get his you-know-what back in his pants before he finds out he doesn't have one anymore." I imagined my dad taking an axe to Joe's "little Joe." Not a good image. Funny, but gross.

I was smart enough to know that leaving them at a time like this was a bad plan, so I order some Chinese take-out, opened a couple of bottles of wine, turned into my seventeen-year-old self and crashed on their couch while Calvin took the spare room. Mom was coming around by the end of the night, and I have the feeling that she is going to be the rock star that is going to get her family through this, because God knows it's not going to be me.

The next time I stopped over at Graham's place, I had some serious ulterior motives. Not only was I checking on my brother, but I was making sure that I got to know his assistant much better. She caught my eye *and gut* the first time I saw her, so I needed to do some serious follow up.

I started the day by putting in some deep reflection by headphoning up with Sting's *Ten Summoner's Tales,* his 1993 release, which was one of my favorite Sting albums. It dawns on me, I need to give you some history with Sting and me. Many people give him flack, and I'm not really sure why. He is a great songwriter, amazing vocalist, and one of the last true rock musicians who cares about his craft. I fell in love with his music when I began playing bass in high school (bass guitar has been my main instrument since I turned 13) and discovered The Police. Most guys want to be the lead singer or lead guitar player, but I am more than happy to stand in the background holding down the groove. Says something about my personality, I'm sure. (I will be some psychiatrist's dream patient someday, but not today). I then followed Sting's solo career, and he has stayed one of my go-to artists when I need some reflective time. I will always love his music, and I will not apologize for that—fight me! So, anyways, I listened to the album and built myself up some deep male self-confidence. I was going to need that if I planned on making some headway with Anne today—in case you were wondering, I am not known for my moves with the ladies.

I arrived at Graham's and found Anne deep in thought on her MacBook. I was a little scared to interrupt her, but she looked up as I walked in and smiled.

"Sorry, but Graham's asleep again, your timing is a little off," she said.

Actually, my timing was perfect. I didn't want to talk to him today, it was all about her. I returned the smile and hoped that I didn't look like a serial killer because sometimes my pictures look a little like that. You know, like I walked into your family photo just after poisoning all of their lemonades. I hoped it wasn't *that* kind of creepy smile. She didn't look repulsed or frightened. So far so good.

"That's okay. I'll hang out if you don't mind. So, you're both a doctoral student and a personal assistant. How does that work?"

I was doing my best to stay cool, but my body language was anything but calm. My foot was tapping constantly, and I'm sure I was involuntarily rubbing my fingers together, as if I was going to start a fire or give myself a blister. This is *really* outside of my comfort zone. Then again, making eye contact was out of my comfort zone. *Who am I kidding?*

"Well, I work for this temp agency that helps college students find part-time work. Being that I am a little older than most of the other students, I get some of the more professional jobs. This wasn't what I was expecting, but I don't mind. I'm trying not to get too attached to your brother because, well, you know, I'm sorry…"

She said all this while updating his schedule spreadsheet, which I could see had both his medical schedule as well as his work stuff he was still trying to maintain, and prepare his dinner of baked chicken and some kind of veggie thing. *She is amazingly efficient.*

"No, no, I get it. I haven't admitted how bad it is to myself yet, but in the back of my mind I know the forecast isn't looking too good."

I must have seemed emotionally vulnerable because, while in the middle of taking care of all of Graham's needs, she stopped, touched my hand and gave me one of the most sincere and deeply sad looks. She didn't even say anything, which is probably good. Because no matter how hard I tried to testosterone-up by listening to Sting (*yeah, that's so manly, Nathan*) I was still pretty raw when I really stopped and thought about my brother's situation. Crying right now would not set me up for future conversations with Anne, though, I would most likely hibernate until retirement.

We continued making small talk until Graham finally came out. He was in good spirits and was looking forward to his dinner. He stopped and made some work-related phone calls all while looking into what appeared to be stocks of some sort on his iPad. I am so lost when it comes to his business, but it looks like a lot of numbers. My mind just starts to wander if I think about it for too long.

Chapter 15

sibling rivalries

Marcie had decided that taking up residency with me and my gang was her best option. (It's not, in case you were wondering.) But she was trying to embed herself into my life. If you remember, Marcie is/was a stay-at-home-ish mom and was becoming a stay-at-home-ish Nathan's sister. This is not a role I wish her to play, nor is she good at. She is overly concerned with my every move and how I am taking care of myself, which, according to her, is not good. She has become part-time Oprah, part-time Martha Stewart, and full-time nightmare. I am really trying to have patience with her, as I know that what she is going through must be terrible, but what I am going through is worse and it needs to stop.

"So, whatcha taking for lunch today?" she asks as my skin begins to crawl.

"Oh, I think I'll get a salad at work today." I have absolutely no intention of getting a salad, but that sounds healthy, and maybe she will let me get away with it.

"Oh, don't do that. I can make you a salad, and it will be so much better than the ones you can get there, and it won't cost you a dime. Let me throw one together for you!" she is smiling as she says this, although I have no idea why. But this is fine, it will save me some money and she can cook pretty well, so maybe it won't be half bad. And honestly, Bert makes our salads, and his hygiene is a little, okay, a lot, questionable.

Frank walks out and begins admiring her workmanship on my salad.

"Are you using Arugula and Romaine in that salad? That looks wonderful." He admired, obviously enjoying having found a culinary kindred spirit.

"Why yes, I am—thanks for noticing. I also marinated the chicken in olive oil, sea salt, crushed peppercorns, and minced garlic. Here, try some."

"Marcie, that's *really* good. I didn't know you like to cook!'

"Oh, I love to, always have. That was one thing Joe never complained about. *Bastard*. Hope young miss pissy pants burns his freaking dinners."

I really just wanted to leave for work and couldn't have cared less what was in my salad. I just wanted this talking to stop and get out the door. Gummy bears and tater tots would have been fine at this point. *For the love of God, please just finish*.

"You know something?" Frank agonizingly extended the

conversation. "I need someone to cater our wedding and I was worried that I was going to have to. Would you like to do it? I mean, I'm pretty fussy and we would have to do quite a bit of research together to get it all perfect."

Oh, please, Frank, *don't* stop talking! *Is he offering to take my sister off of my shoulders for a while?* Oh yes, this could be exactly what I, I mean, *she* needs. Oh, you perfect, short, muscular, gay man! *Probably should keep that thought in my head, but please say yes, Marcie.*

"That sounds great," Marcie replied.

The most wonderful three words I have heard in a long time. "I have never done anything that big, so I will need some help, but I know some other moms that would probably love to help. Oh, Frank, this is really exciting." Waiting for the eternal salad had become well worth the effort. It was a lot of work standing there pretending to care about their conversation while waiting for a salad I may or may not eat.

I finally escaped and made my way to work where I spent the next eight hours in the company of Bert and Jessica. We talked endlessly about music. Typical day for me, but usually the banter is inside my head, so this was a nice change of pace. I had to check myself a couple of times to make sure I allowed them to talk as well. During the day, I found my thoughts drifting back to Anne and what my next move was going to be. Actually, I haven't had a first move, so maybe I needed to start there. Was this kind of creepy? I mean, this girl is taking care of my dying brother and I'm trying to scheme up ways to get her out on a date. *I'm really not a good person, am I?* Well, the heart can't help what the heart wants, and right now the heart wants me to come up with a way to ask Anne out. *That is what needed to happen.* So, the only way to do that was to see her again. *I will stop by Graham's tomorrow.*

I came home to find Frank and Marcie knee deep in recipes and Pinterest decorating ideas. It was great to see her spirits so high, but I was beginning to worry about how much separation she was putting between herself and her kids. Joe had crushed her soul, but if she wanted to remain a good mom, she needed to get back in that saddle. And that's not just me getting sick of her being around, that's me wanting to make sure my sister doesn't turn into a deadbeat mom. But that nerve is still a little raw, so I'll wait to bring it up. I had bigger issues to worry about, like what I was going to wear tomorrow to see Anne. Look, my siblings all dropped stuff on me this past month, I need a little "Nathan Time."

Chapter 16

try not to be weird, nathan

I arrived at Graham's house after lunch, giving him time to get his treatment in the morning and recover. I entered the front door and found him in his living room. Man, he was getting more and more frail by the day. I'm glad, in more ways than one, that he had hired Anne to take care of him, as I don't think any of us could have. I didn't notice my mom standing in the kitchen for a minute. She just smiled when we made eye contact.

"Hey, Nathan," Graham whispered. This was the same voice I had heard from him the last time I stopped by, and I was hoping he would have sounded better.

"How's it going?" I tried to sound as normal as possible, but I could tell I wasn't really pulling it off. "You need Mom to come help you out today? What happened to that assistant of yours?" Still not smooth, but I don't think he noticed.

I'm really not trying to take advantage of his sickness, but my suave dating skills need all the help they can get, and I know my brother, he would do the same to me.

"She ran an errand, Romeo. Don't worry she'll be back any minute."

Was I that obvious? Damn it, Nathan!

"Oh, does Nathan have his eye on little Anne?" Mom joined in as she entered from the kitchen.

Please don't call her "little Anne," Mom, that sounds even creepier than I know I already am.

"I don't know what you're talking about. She has been very helpful, and she seems to brighten up my brother when she's around," I replied, staying as neutral as possible.

"Really?" Graham perked up. "I was thinking the same thing about her in regards to you. All I know is, you haven't been to my house this much since I've owned it."

"Oh yeah, well you haven't had cancer this much since you've owned it either," I retorted sarcastically, winking and smiling at him so he would know I was busted.

"Well, good thing I have it now. If nothing else, maybe my crap will help your love life." Graham laughed bigger than I had heard in quite some time, and I hoped that maybe it did lift his spirits. Mom didn't like this type of talk, I could tell, but she was the type that had to immerse herself into a situation that she didn't like in order to come out the other side with her wits intact. If she sat around all day denying his sickness existed, she would never get out of a very dark place if he got worse. So, if she puts herself in his presence and can even begin to joke about it, this is going to be her way of coping and dealing with the reality that I was becoming more and more afraid was facing my brother.

Finally, Anne arrived with a car full of really healthy groceries, and I found myself thinking that maybe Marcie was onto something, maybe I did need to eat better. I helped her bring everything in and did my best with trying to make small talk. Mom took Graham out back so he could get some sun on the patio.

"Wow, do you always eat this healthy? Or is this just for my bro?" I was initiating small talk, so bear with me. It's not in my wheelhouse.

"Yeah, I'm extremely picky about what I eat, but I'll tell you what, I am never sick, and I feel way better when I eat right. Are you a healthy eater like Graham?"

I had no idea since I had no idea how Graham eats, but I'm going to infer that she assumes he is healthy, and I can honestly tell you that I try but have failed epically many times.

"Well, I have good days and bad days. But my roommate Frank is a vegetarian, and he keeps Claire and I on track as best he can."

"Is Claire your girlfriend?"

"No, no, no," I stated as emphatically as possible. I really may need to rethink my living arrangements as I wonder if my best friend being female is working against my mojo.

"We are all just friends. Claire and I went to college together in Pittsburgh and we met frank down here through a mutual friend."

"What school did you guys go to?"

"I went to Duquesne and she went to Pitt, but we were

both involved in the musical theater scene up there and that's how we met." Great! A platonic female roommate and musical theater, now I'm on Frank's team. *This is a disaster— and is exactly why I can't make small talk!*

The banter went back and forth as I tried to convince her of my heterosexuality. I learned that she had graduated from UMass and was now getting her doctorate at Rollins College here in Winter Park. She was going to try and open up a school she told me.

"I want to open up a school for gifted children. I feel like they are getting lost in the public-school system. But that's a ways off just yet."

"So, you're like Professor X?"

"Yes, but without the physical mutations." She laughed.

Oh. My. God. Did she really just get my X-Men reference and not miss a beat with a comical retort? I love her.

The day continued, and I tried to flirt a little more and more. I'm really not sure how well I did with that. She laughed when I hoped she would and never really stared at me like I was a complete moron, which, when it comes to conversations with the opposite gender, is a small miracle for me. Then came a small bombshell.

"So, why are you still just a barista? Are you going back to school, or what is your plan?" she asked with sincere innocence.

This is where they get you. This is how they measure you up for being good dating material or not. What is your plan? What are your life goals? Well, to answer you honestly, Anne, I plan on purchasing as many records as humanly possible in my lifetime and spending my other free time learning about the minutia of all my favorite rock bands. Then, I will sit around and tell people how bad their taste is in music. *I sound like a dreamboat, don't I?* Not my best answer, so let me try a different approach.

"I guess it's just what I'm doing right now. I know that I want to do more in the music field, but I just don't know what yet."

"That's cool."

She said it like she actually meant it, and I honestly didn't feel one vibe of judgment from her at all. This was no mere mortal of a female. This was a goddess.

Chapter 17

life and trying not to adult

So, yeah, I'm not going to say that the whole, "What are you going to do when you grow up, Nathan?" conversation with Anne yesterday, doesn't have me a little freaked out. I mean, I never really cared what other people thought of me and, how or if, they judged me. But now I do. What do I do with that? All of a sudden, there was this person whose opinion I suddenly find myself valuing. And this wasn't a musical opinion, either. This was like being on completely foreign soil. The panic was two-fold. Not only did I find myself caring about her opinion, I realized that I had no idea how to answer that question. *What do I want to do for the foreseeable future?* I know I enjoyed my job right now, but for no other reason than there were absolutely no responsibilities. I had avoided the actual growing up part that came with the growing number attached to your birthday.

I was okay with that. I mean, look at all of my musical heroes. All of them seemed like they stopped maturing after age eighteen. All of them except McCartney. He is in his seventies and he is now approaching thirty in maturity years. But then again, I'm not a multi-millionaire. Maybe I need a slightly better plan than winging it through life. Okay, but this girl. *Why should I worry about my life's direction for this girl?* I can argue with myself like the best of them, but in the end, I do really care.

But I also needed to help Frank get this wedding together in about five and a half months, and he has asked me to be his best man. Although, I'm not sure how that works in a gay wedding. Am I the best man or the man-of-honor? I don't care. Whatever it's called, I want to make sure that I am there for Frank and be whatever he needs. His conversation with Gary's family hit a rocky shore and Gary was pretty much sailing on his own. We will pull together and get this off the ground, but it will take a lot of work.

"Frank, I have begun putting together a playlist for your wedding. I will go over the details with you later, but it's going to be awesome."

"Yeah, that's great. I have some ideas about that, but I'm sure what you have is cute." Frank was always a little hesitant about my tastes. While we were completely on the same page on eighties classical alternative, Frank was very wrong when it came to his thoughts on pop music. Thank God I was here to help, because he was going to need it. *I will not let him down.* I will provide the perfect wedding soundtrack, and he will find himself eternally grateful to me for it. It's how I roll.

"My biggest concern is the guest list," Frank lamented. "Gary has basically no support, and I don't want him to feel bad, but I have a big family and they are really supportive of our life choices, so this is going to be awkward."

"Well, I suggest we just seat people wherever, both in the church and at the reception, so there's no reason to be worried about who is with whom and it will all look good." That was my best "best man" advice (best he was going to get). I was completely uninvolved in Marcie's wedding and that was one of only four weddings I have been to in my whole life. I have been to about two dozen funerals, so I've got that covered, but weddings are not my thing.

"Well, we'll work it out later, but next week you need to come with me and pick out tuxes. Your sister has been a complete dream with the menu, and I think we are going to have one of the most creative and delicious vegan weddings ever."

Oh great, vegan wedding. I'll make sure to eat before I go. But, if anyone was able to polish that turd of a menu, it was going to be Marcie. I had seen her earlier today and I'll tell you, she looks great. We chatted about the kids and it sounds like even though Joe does have things under control, she is going to spend the weekends with them and help out with taxiing them to and from daycare. I mean, Joe is a complete schmuck, but he can't raise the kids alone. I would have lost a lot of respect for my sister if she had done that.

I decided since Frank had Marcie under control and Graham had Anne helping him out, I would touch base with Calvin later in the week. For now, I needed some "me time."

I believed that going for a long walk was what the doctor ordered, so I headed out the door. On my way out, Claire stopped me and asked what I was up to and if she could tag along. There are times in life when you do that internal sigh and think to yourself, "I just wanted some quiet," but you realize that this is one of your closest friends and it would do you both some good to hang out. So, we took off down the road with the innocent and sole intention of heading to the record store. I knew there I could find something to grab that would take my mind off life for a bit, and Claire was always game to join me.

"So, I'm thinking about asking Anne out for coffee. What do you think?" I figured there was no sense in beating around the bush, and if anyone was going to give it to me straight, it was Claire.

"Is that the chick taking care of your brother? Isn't that a little weird? And didn't you say she was like rally super organized? That is so *not you*, although maybe she could help you out in that respect, God knows no one else can. Are you sure you can keep up? You don't need more disappointment in your life right now, Nathan."

"Yeah, she's got a lot of energy, but I kinda like that. She keeps me on my toes. And no, it's not weird, I mean we are two grown adults who are connected by a difficult situation, but I think we can make it past that."

"What do you mean "make it past that"? Are you actually thinking that there would be more than one date? What has gotten into you? You, sly dog."

I explained to Claire that while I had no idea where these

feelings were all coming from, I was suddenly and completely intoxicated by this woman. That she had, with her spunk and peppiness and purpose-driven attitude, brightened my day every time I stopped by Graham's, and that for the first time in a long time, I really wanted to get to know someone and spend actual time with that someone. This was a new and adventurous direction for me, but I couldn't help it. I was determined that I would move forward and ask this girl out, no matter how much it terrified me and no matter how great the chance of rejection was. I could do it!

We reached Rock n Roll Heaven, and Rick proceeded to flirt with Claire, like he always does. It's really creepy. Claire is a peach and lets him say flattering things to her. But, it's like she does it because she feels sorry for him. Poor Rick. He's a perfectly normal, probably good-looking guy with a really successful record shop, but no woman will ever take him seriously because he is so off-putting. He has a huge ego and always directs customers to purchase records that are *so bad* no one should be allowed to listen to them. He should be fined for inflicting such inhumane noise pollution on their ears. I walk away knowing she can handle herself, and I wander over to the Queen section. I realize that I do not own their 1980 classic album *The Game*. "Play the Game," "Crazy Little Thing Called Love," "Another One Bites the Dust," "Save Me." What great songs! *How do I not own this?* Well, it was decided. I was going to go home and lose myself in my headphones with a couple of Diet Pepsi's and all would be good. I could see from Claire's exasperated expression that it was time for me to save her. I'm glad I was able to make this choice quickly. Usually, it would take me an hour, at least, and I could tell it was time to go; she was done with Rick and his musical idiocy.

I paid for my selection while their ridiculous banter continued, as if I wasn't even there. (You're welcome, Rick, as I help pay your rent here!) As we exited the store, I could almost feel Claire's relief.

"Funny you bought *that* album. Rick is taking me to see Bohemian Rhapsody at the Enzian this Friday night! Funny how that works, huh? You got a record, and I got a date—all connected by Freddie Mercury. I love how music always ties our worlds together, don't you?"

"A date? *With Rick?* What are you thinking? *He's a moron!* Are you even listening to yourself? When has he ever given one good piece of musical advice? I mean, *c'mon, Claire!* What do you even see in him?" I was lost. This did not make any sense to me. How could someone as smart and cool as Claire possibly think that a music nimrod like Rick was worth going on a date with? I needed to save her from possible potential relationship doom.

"Really, Nathan? He's really cute, and he was the one who first told you about the rare R.E.M. bootleg recording from the 1986 concert at Syria Mosque from the Life's Rich Pageant tour. You didn't even know that recording existed, but Rick did, and he knew you and I went to school in the 'burgh and may have been interested in that history because that's something musically nerdy *you* would like. Or how about that time he had the copy of Neil Young's Harvest Moon that he saved for you because it was the only vinyl copy in town?"

"I hated that record, by the way. Even a blind squirrel finds a nut once in a while, but that doesn't make Rick datable. He is so not your type."

"How about you leave my dating choices to me, Mr. E-Harmony. Last time I checked, Romeo, you weren't knocking it out of the park. You are just jealous because Rick is the only person on the planet who challenges your rock and roll minutiae knowledge scale of useless information. HE is a *really cool* guy, and I am excited to go out with him. I've honestly had a crush on him for about a year now, so I'm glad he's finally asked me."

This is so deeply disturbing. I'm so glad I've got some good, classic musical perfection to listen to tonight, I'm going to need it. Now I have to worry about Claire. How is she going to change if she is tainted by the musical stupidity that is Rick? It's okay, my headphones are on, my Diet Pepsi is cold, and my eyes are closed. Thirty plus minutes to get my thoughts together. Musical meditation. I think I will listen to this one at least three times through tonight.

Chapter 18

here goes nothing

Well, Claire's Friday night date has come and gone, and I occupied myself by working as many hours as possible. It does a soul good to make some money and not dwell on your roommate's bad life choices. Actually, her life choices are so bad that she is going on a second date. I opened up to Frank about the seriousness of this issue and he is obviously too preoccupied with his upcoming nuptials to be bothered by the immensity of it.

"Let her be, dude. Don't worry about it. She seems really happy. Why are you trying to screw it up?"

He is obviously delirious. I'll just have to keep taking care of life by myself.

My thoughts are now turning to Anne. I need to finally get up the courage to ask her to join me for dinner, or a coffee, or a movie. If I had to be honest, which I would never admit to Claire, Rick had actually given me the courage to finally take the next steps. I mean, if a putz like him can get Claire to not only go out with him once, but twice, surely, I could at least ask Anne out for a date.

I had called Anne to see if she needed me to pick anything up on my way over this afternoon and she said that she could actually use some groceries and gave me a small list. I had also wanted to spend some time with Calvin, and I figured, two birds, right? I picked him up on the way, so he could occupy Graham while I had some time to talk to Anne. Plus, I honestly felt like the three of us being together was good for Graham as well. He seemed to really enjoy family being around right now.

We grabbed Anne's list of stuff and headed over to see our brother. Calvin was in great spirits as his church was doing really well, and he was a new man with an open and fresh lifestyle. He was also looking forward to Frank's upcoming ceremony as it was going to be his first same-sex service and he seemed proud to be able to do this for my friend, which was really sweet.

We pulled into Graham's and brought in the groceries. Graham was seated at his kitchen table and it was obvious this treatment was taking its toll. He was looking more frail, and his skin seemed to be hanging on his bones, but his eyes were still bright.

"Thanks for stopping by, guys. I'm getting sick of looking at Anne and these four walls."

Anne walked in at that point and shot right back at him, "Well, you're getting a little stale too, Mr. Smythe." They both smiled at each other, and I knew that this was a good combination for Graham as he was going through this mess.

We settled the food where it needed to be, and I asked Anne if we could chat for a minute. I left Calvin with Graham who he was bringing up to speed about his congregation and their wonderful acceptance of his new out-and-proud personal life. Anne and I walked out the back-patio slider, and I felt like I just needed to start right in.

"I know you have been working crazy hours here and I was wondering if I could take you out for dinner or a movie at some point?" This is where it usually falls apart for me, and, believe it or not, I actually knew how to handle that denial better than you might expect. So, I got my best, "It's okay, I understand," line ready.

"That sounds great. I could really use a night out, and I haven't been on a date for a few months. I would love to. Thank you for asking, Nathan. I must admit, I'm a little surprised, I thought I was annoying you."

Wow, she was already calling it a "date"! *Why was she thinking she was annoying me?* Oh well, things not to worry about.

"Annoying me? No way. I've actually been really nervous about asking you out."

We decided that a mid-week date was best since I would be working on the weekend and she was free tomorrow. The choice was a movie and dinner at Chuy's as we both love Mexican food. We went back inside. Obviously, I was on cloud nine and I really couldn't contain it.

"What's up with you two?" Graham teased.

"Well, your brother just asked me out on a date, and I said yes, so you are on your own tomorrow night."

"Are you kidding? Nathan are you scamming on my nurse? Did it take me dying for you to finally get a date?" Both Graham and Calvin were finding this very amusing. But that was okay; I was going out with Anne.

"Well, you handed me lemons and I made the lemonade. Yes, I am taking your precious Anne away from you for a night. You better call Mom or Marcie to come and take care of you, buster."

"Actually," Calvin interjected, "I have nothing going on tomorrow, and I just purchased season six of *Game of Thrones*. I could bring it over and we could do dinner together. What do you think, old man?"

Graham's face lit up, and I loved the fact that Calvin was really coming around and seeming more and more human every day. But, then again, I really didn't care what happened as long as it didn't change the fact that I was taking Anne out.

Chapter 19

the dating is the hardest part

So, I'm about to take Anne out for our first dinner together, and I'm about to puke. This is probably not a good sign for my night ahead. I need to pull myself together, but I am nervous as heck. There is a good reason, too. I mean, I haven't been out for a while and I know how important first impressions are. And I'm not known for making great ones. You're shocked, I know. But that was then, this is now. I will pick her up, we will get to the restaurant, and all will be great. *Deep breaths.*

Frank was not helping the matter much with his constant running commentary on the subject.

"You sure you remember what do to on a date? What's it been, like a decade since you last went out? You're wearing that?" *Please make him stop.* Yes, I'm wearing this. A classic combination of Levi's and a button-down. Can't miss.

I'm trying to impress her, not you, Frank. Claire wasn't home before I left which was also a good thing, as I have not been very positive about her dating Rick. I still don't see what she sees in him, but whatever floats her boat. She'll see things my way *eventually*.

I got some gas and a small bouquet of flowers on my way over to pick her up. She lives in downtown Winter Park, which is actually not very far from my place at all, and real convenient while she finishes up at Rollins College. She greets me at the door and looks absolutely stunning.

"C'mon in," she says through the screen door, "but watch out for the cats." I spot a big orange tabby and a smaller grey cat wandering about. I love cats. This is getting more perfect every day.

"They are adorable, what're their names?"

"The orange one is Einstein and the gray one is Navi."

"Like from Legend of Zelda, Navi?"

"Yup, my little brother was a huge fan of the game, and I used to play with him all the time." She laughed.

Her nerd cred is getting better and better. Little does she know she is about to date the Nerd King. Aside from my attempt to achieve encyclopedic knowledge of certain rock bands, I am also a hopeless fan of Star Trek and a super tech junkie. I don't know who gets more of my money, Rock n Roll Heaven or Apple. Well, Apple gets more money, but I spend more time at…never mind.

We leave her place after spending some quality time with her cats and proceed to Chuys, which, ironically, happens to be both hers and my favorite Mexican establishment in town. She is not sure about the flowers, and I worry that I may have overstepped my boundaries there, but go big or go home, right?

The restaurant is not too busy tonight and we find a seat right off.

"So, you pretty much know my whole family and all of our drama, right now, so tell me about you. Who is this mystery woman taking care of my brother?"

"Well, I told you I went to UMass for my undergrad, UCF for my Master's and I'm finishing up my Ph.D. at Rollins right now. My study is in Gifted Education with a focus on Special Needs students, mostly because my little brother is on the autistic spectrum combined with an extremely high IQ. It's called Twice-Exceptional and those are the kids I want to focus on; where I want to make my biggest difference. I've seen how misunderstood and ignored my brother has been, and I want nothing more than to be an advocate for these kids. They are always being mislabeled and sometimes even extremely mistreated by their teachers. I can't stand it, and I will do something to stop it where I can. Sorry, I'm getting a little heated, but I'm so passionate about this, you wouldn't even begin to understand."

No, I probably wouldn't understand, but boy I wanted to. I wanted nothing more than to become part of her world, but this is going to be an uphill battle for me. I'm never going to live in her intellectual atmosphere; she is way too far up there. The best I can hope for is to charm her with my winning personality and that has a checkered track record at best. We talked and talked and talked for what seemed like only thirty minutes, but it was actually three hours. We had missed our movie, and I couldn't have been happier. We had filled each other's heads with stories of our pasts and hopes for our futures. But now I was needing to make sure that those futures collided. We moved from talking at the restaurant, to talking in the car, to walking around Park Avenue, just down from her place. Finally, she needed to get home.

"This has been a really great night," Anne said quietly. "Thank you so much for everything. It's good to have someone to converse with that actually listens. Sometimes my friends just look at me like I'm crazy."

"Trust me, I know the feeling." I could have listened all night.

"But I need to be back to Graham's early tomorrow for his treatment. It's his last one for a while. So, I probably should be getting home."

I drove her back to her place, and we talked a little about Graham for the first time all night. She is very worried about him, as we all are, but coming from her it sounded so much more grave. She let me kiss her goodnight, which was the perfect ending to this whole event.

Let me tell you something about that first kiss. You know when they show fireworks going off in the movies, it was nothing like that. It was perfect. Fireworks fade, but perfection doesn't. It was the kind of kiss that you knew you had to have again, you wouldn't and couldn't live without it, and that you never needed to have one from anyone else for the rest of your life. Perfection.

I drove home on top of the world. But I forgot to ask her if I could see her again! What an idiot! It's okay, I tried to get myself to stop panicking. I know where she works, and I'm free to visit her there at any point. I need to make sure I call her tomorrow. Or was that too soon? Maybe I should wait until the weekend. But is that too long? Ah, crap. Perfection tainted by my neurotic anxiety. Wonderful.

I got home to find Claire and Rick cuddling on my couch. Gross. *Why must you torture me so, Claire!?*

"How was your date, Nate?" Rick asked. This was his attempt at trying to be funny. It's not funny. Calling me Nate is also not cute coming from you, Rick! And that whole rhyming thing you just did? Don't. Please, just don't. That is something I would do, and now I will never do it again in my life as it sounds stupid. But maybe it was just because it came out of his stupid face.

"It went great. We had a really good time." I managed to get that much out because I was determined I wasn't going to downplay the wonderfulness of the evening because of Rick.

"Couldn't of been *that* good if you're here and not there."

Rick was a pig. Yes, Rick it *could* have been that good because we talked all night. Just because you are trying to get into Claire's pants (good luck with that, by the way), doesn't mean we all have zero class. There are some gentlemen still left in the world! And Claire is not going to fall for your crudeness, you know, she is way above that. If only my mouth worked with my brain, I'd have even less friends.

"C'mon, let's leave him alone. He has better things to do than listen to you razz him." And with that, Claire led

Rick back to her bedroom. *Are you kidding me!?* Please tell me he is not going to be here in the morning. *I cannot face that stupidhead in the morning!*

Chapter 20

morning after dilemmas

The next morning was nothing short of a disaster. I still had thoughts of Anne floating around in my head and what my next plan of action would be...Was I going to call? Stop by? Text her? Wait until next week? *Ugh-this is too hard.* But then, just when life couldn't possibly get any worse, I walked into MY kitchen to see Rick standing there in his boxers, drinking MY coffee out of MY Sun Studios collectable coffee mug! *What fresh hell was this?* I was not in the right mental state to deal with him in my reality this morning. Must. Move. On.

"Morning sunshine," he said, like he was *my* lover.

Please let me have an aneurysm right now.

"Hey man, how's it going?" I replied, pretending to care.

"Pretty good. Pretty good." He winked at me.

I hate that almost as much as I hate another guy touching

me. Maybe it's just because it's Rick. I decided that not replying was my best course of action. I proceeded to gather my stuff and head out the door so I could get to work on time.

Traffic was nice and open on my way to the shop and this really helped me to clear my thoughts. I had my really peppy new playlist going featuring Matthew Sweet, R.E.M., and some early Beatles. Nothing like "She Loves You" followed by a little "Radio Free Europe" to make you smile. I needed to get my head wrapped around this Anne situation, and all I keep doing is avoiding it in my head. I know that I really like her. I mean, I REALLY like her. I also know that I have made other women feel nervous by seeming too clingy and desperate, so I have to watch my pacing. I was really hoping to talk to Claire about this, but her recent life choices are making me wonder if she is my best sounding board.

I arrived at work, and the only person I had to converse with was Bert. This is not the person from whom you really want to get dating advice. His personality screams *I have not had much success with the women folk.* I mean, I am no Johnny Depp, but if I needed to raise the bar of my dating life, getting his advice was not the best course of action.

I could see the look in his eyes, that he was in the mood to talk today. Bert has that way about him. He either wants to keep to himself and not utter a sound, or he is going to gab and gab and gab. Well, I could use the distraction, so here goes nothing.

"Hey, Bert, how's it going? What's new?"

"Well," he said, looking like he couldn't contain himself.

"I have spent the last two days watching the complete three seasons of *Star Trek: The Original Series*. There is nothing like some Shatner and Nimoy to get your creative juices flowing. Did you know the command uniforms were actually green and not yellow? That they only appear yellow because of the lighting used on the set? Not many people outside of Trekkies know that, but now you know it."

Yes, not many people know it because not many people care. But I actually did know that because, as I have told you, I have some major nerd tendencies. But I did not want to go down that road, and I wanted to stop having the conversation. So, what was I going to do? I was going to ask him for relationship advice and that should shut down this dialogue.

"Bert, let me ask you something. First, yes, I knew that about the uniforms, but it is still a cool piece of trivia, but what is your opinion on calling a girl back after a first date? Should I call her today? Tomorrow? I went out with this chick last night; actually, she is my brother Graham's assistant, and she is amazing! So, I don't know if I should call her, if I should stop by and see her, or if I should just lay low and wait it out a bit. What are your thoughts?"

This is where I expect Bert's brain to explode. I just vomited more words at him than I have ever spoken to him in one shift. I totally derailed his train of thought and I asked him for female advice. This should keep our talking to a minimum and let us work the rest of the shift in relative silence. I saw him look down for a minute, probably not wanting to embarrass himself.

"Well, when I first started dating Gracie," he started, (Who the hell is Gracie? I have never ever heard of this person! Is he hallucinating and should I be concerned?) "we went out once and I didn't call her back for a week. This was a *huge* mistake, and if I could ever take it back I would. I should have called her either the next day or no later than two days later. Actually, if I was to recommend something, I would text her with something sweet today, not too pushy, not too creepy, but something nice telling her how much you enjoyed going out with her last night, reminding her that you would like to see her again. But, that's just my opinion."

Freaking Twilight Zone Thursday! First, I start the day with Rick in his skivvies and now I am getting Dr. Phil level advice from Bert The Love Master! Sometimes I don't k now how I survive myself and the people around me. They keep jumping from personality to personality and I can't keep up. I don't like when people surprise me. They need to live in the little box that I like to keep them in, so that I know how to utilize them in my life. Discovering that Bert is a fountain of love knowledge, I will never again see him as the "I live in my closet and watch films all day" kid. And again, *who the hell* is this Gracie?

"You know something, Bert, that is *really* great advice. And, to be fair, I really didn't expect that from you, so thanks." I think he smiled with a more sincere smile that I had ever seen. I kinda felt good about it.

So, on my first break, I decided that texting her was my best plan. I sucked when it came to talking on the phone, so I needed to keep it as cool as possible and this requires me to keep my mouth shut.

Me: *I had a great time last night. I was hoping that I could see you again sometime.*

After an eternal ten minutes, which goes completely against texting etiquette:

Anne: *I would love that. And thanks, I had a great time too. Call me later!*

So, it is settled, Bert is a genius. Without his help I would have been paralyzed with fear and indecision. I finished my shift in such a great mood that I was going to have to revamp my playlist again. This was going to need to be stepped up a level. Up to a level that I have never gone to before in my musical history. I was going to make a romance playlist. That's right, A ROMANCE playlist. I was woozy with anticipation.

I arrived back at my place to find Calvin, Frank, and Claire deep in wedding talk. Since I was the best man, I knew that I needed to step up and be there more for Frank. I was beginning to feel like I was letting him down.

"What's up, guys and gal?" I interjected, hoping not to feel too left out.

"Well," Frank started, "I need to pick a place for the reception, but the garden that I wanted will not allow us to have our dinner there. They said that they have to answer to their board of directors and they weren't ready to make that bold of a step."

I could tell by Frank's body language that this bothered him deeply. He was still not used to getting treated as if his lifestyle choice was a plague of some sort. He didn't understand (and neither do I) why people just can't let you love who you want to love? These types of injustices made me angry, and when they hurt my friends it made it worse.

"Well, fuck them!" I replied indignantly. "You don't need them. You know what, Graham has a gorgeous backyard, and I can ask him if we could have it there. He has plenty of room, considering you guys were only thinking of having about a hundred people. We can totally make this happen, save you some money, and not have to deal with any of these assholes."

"That's a great idea," Calvin said enthusiastically.

"Nathan, if you really think he is going to be up for it? I don't want to trouble him right now."

"I'll deal with him, but I think this could be something that may make him happy to do. And he really could use some of that right now." Not only that, it gave me a great reason to go visit Anne tomorrow.

Chapter 21

smythe weddings, inc.

The next morning, Calvin and I drove across town to Graham's place. But first let me bring you up to speed on the events of yesterday evening with Anne. I totally forgot to call her. If I haven't made this clear in the past, I am quite the champ when it comes to dating. I couldn't even get my thoughts straight yesterday, finally got some guru-like advice from Bert, texted her (she TOLD me to call her) and I got so caught up in the events of the day with Frank that a few drinks and one Abbey Road LP later, I was spent. Anne, I apologize already, but you've got a long road ahead of you if you continue to date me.

We found Graham sitting in his living room covered in blankets, even though his thermostat read eighty degrees. He looked like he was dozing, but his eyes opened when he heard us walk in.

"Hey there, my dudes," he barely gasped.

I could tell that conversation for him was going to be painful, so I told him he could just sit there and nod. I went through the whole story about Frank and the homophobic garden owners and it did not take any convincing for Graham to agree to let us use his yard for their wedding. As pompous of an ass as Graham could be back in the day, he was always very aware of social injustices and did what he could, when he could, to make things right. Man, between Calvin officiating the ceremony, Marci cooking for it, and Graham providing the reception area, we Smythes have got it going on for wedding organization. Actually, I'm doing jack crap, but hey, I brought them all together, and I'm gonna look great in whatever tux or gown Frank puts me in.

Anne arrived just as we were getting ready to go. Graham decided he needed a nap, so Anne and I went out to the back porch to take a look at the grounds for Frank's upcoming nuptials. Calvin answered some emails on his phone and watched over Graham.

"Sorry, I forgot to call yesterday. But once all this went down with Frank, I kind of got lost in the whole thing," I told her. I mean, it didn't really take all that long, but you know how sometimes one thing leads to another and then the whole conversation started with Claire and Rick and "what was the best Beatles album (Sgt. Pepper's) and how good was Abbey Road (really good, but not the best)" thing started between Rick and I. I couldn't just let him continue to live his life misinformed.

"That's okay, but I was starting to think maybe you didn't

really have a good time." She smirked. If there was anything she could tell about me right now, it was that I was incredibly excited to see her as I was almost tripping over myself trying to talk to her. She *knew* I had a good time.

"Is it possible to see you again this week?" Even though I was pretty confident of the answer, I couldn't help but be nervous. I was actually amazed at how nervous I was. Like "not able to make eye contact with her" nervous.

"Yes! I was hoping maybe later in the week? Graham is getting to where he is needing me to stay a little longer every day, but we actually have real nurses starting with him on Thursday, so maybe Friday night? I just want to make sure he is settled."

I was so excited I think that I forgot to answer her with my outside voice because I just stared at her for what seemed like fifteen minutes without saying anything, but I'm sure it was more like five seconds. She finally gave me "the look" and it brought me back to the present. We agreed that Friday sounded wonderful, and we decided to catch the theater department's performance of "The Hound of The Baskervilles" at her campus. As a self-diagnosed Anglophile, anything Sherlockian was great for me. I suggested an English restaurant nearby to complete the theme of the evening. I would begin on a British Invasion playlist as soon as I got home to top the night off.

As we drove back to my place, I could tell there was something troubling Calvin. He isn't necessarily a shallow fella, but he wasn't hiding the fact that something was troubling him.

"Something bothering you, Cal?" I tried to ask as lightly as possible.

"Well, not bothering me, per se, but I need to get something off of my chest, and for some reason, you seem to be in the firing line of that lately—sorry." He laughed as he said this, but I prepared for the worst. I mean, I shouldn't honestly worry, with the past few months I've had, how bad could it be, right? Never say that, even to yourself.

"Well, after coming out to you and the family, I'm starting to feel like I need to be fully transparent about everything. I hope you're okay with me telling you this, but here goes. I've been in a relationship for a little while now with a guy named Paul, and while I was going to keep this a secret, everything has just fallen into place. I mean, there's nothing too serious yet, but with the freedom that I am feeling in my life, I don't want there to be anything that I keep from my family. I lived in shame for long enough, and that chapter of my life is over. I'm not ready for you guys to meet him yet, but I think that time may be coming soon, and I don't want to surprise you."

Surprise me, hell I'm Captain Blindside lately! Every time I turn around one of my siblings is tossing a proverbial bombshell in my direction. I'm barely keeping this crap together, Calvin! *When did it become a good idea to throw your emotions at Nathan?* I'll tell you when, NEVER! I'm the introverted, quiet, keep to myself guy in the family. Not the "hey, here's our crazy laundry" guy! Good lord!

"Well, thank you for trusting me enough to tell me, and whenever you feel ready, know that it's no big deal to me."

It really is not a big deal to me, I just have to keep getting used to these new lives all of my family is living. It's a crazy world when your parents all of sudden seem the most normal part of your life.

We kept conversing about his new man, Paul, and I found out that he is a manager of a Books-A-Million and leads a pretty laid-back life. I am hoping for the best for my brother, because he has been alone for too long and in hiding for even longer, so any happiness that came his way would be great.

After dropping Calvin off, I got back to the apartment and found that it was just Claire, Frank, and me in the house. Between Marcie, Gary, and now Rick (still not happy about that), spending an increased amount of time with us, recently, it has felt like we have a revolving door. But it was just The Three Musketeers. This felt good. I walked over to the turntable and put on U2's classic *The Joshua Tree*. I get accused by other music snobs for liking some very "mainstream" stuff. But, my argument is that an album like *Joshua Tree* is huge, because it's *great*. That doesn't make it less cool. Just go listen to it. It drives me crazy the music/fil/book snobs that only feel like the most obscure, indie releases are worth their time. Sometimes, a band is obscure because they suck. Sometimes you find a jewel in the rough, but a lot of times you find crap. I digress, but as soon as the record started, I saw both Claire and Frank start bobbing and grooving to it. My peeps. We listened to three more full-length U2 albums that afternoon before deciding that is was time for some food, as it was almost seven o'clock. The Mill in Winter Park was our choice for their local brewed amber beer and pizza.

I loved the vibe of that place, and it was always slow on a Monday night.

We found a quiet booth in the corner so we were able to converse and plan Frank's wedding and discuss the bad idea of Rick, while not really being seen or heard by the other customers. I mean, honestly, this hip establishment is bound to have other clients of Rock n Roll Heaven, and I couldn't have anyone think that one of my best pals in the world has done the horizontal mambo with Mushhead Rick.

"What do you even see in that guy?" I argued. "You realize that he is my arch enemy, right?"

"How do you even have an arch enemy, Nathan? He is a sweet and a really nice guy. You need to shut up and give him a chance. And by the way, I don't give a shit what you think, I'm still dating him," Claire said, way more sternly than she should have.

She is not thinking straight, I'll give her some time.

"She's right, you know," Frank interjected, even though I did not ask him. "He treats Claire really nice and he and I had a great conversation about photography the other night. Did you know he has some original Annie Leibovitz's prints? That's some classic stuff!"

Frank was obviously delusional with wedding planning and nothing he said should or could be taken seriously at this point. These two are exhausting me and I needed to change the subject, but Claire was just about to do that. I wished she hadn't.

"Isn't that Anne over there?" she asked, seemingly innocently, but I'm still not sure, it may have been sadistic.

Why yes, yes it is. And she isn't alone. Not only wasn't she alone, but she was with a very distinguished looking guy, probably in his late thirties. And she was smiling. Way too much. And I knew this wasn't anyone she was related to because she just told me they all lived out of state, and from her description of them, this wasn't one of them. This guy looked like an academic, not the hard-working blue collar family she came from. He looked like he hadn't been outside for about a lifetime. But they were enjoying a glass of wine and seeming way too happy about it. The Mill wine selection wasn't that good to be this happy about. But I wasn't about to imagine that she was having a great conversation over there. That was not going to enter my mind at this point in time. I will just ignore it.

"Are you going to say hi, or do you think she's on a date?" Frank asked.

"Go over to say 'hi'. *Are you kidding me?* I have inadvertently humiliated myself way more than the average human. I am not about to do it on purpose! How stupid do I look? Don't answer that, Claire," I protested.

This was the worst thing ever. I couldn't even eat my pizza, but I finished way more than my share of beer. How could she do this to me? Why would she do this to me? I mean, she was watching over my dying brother, for crying out loud! Why would she be out on a date with this Professor Ballsack? I mean, she just asked me to see her again this Friday! If she's going to date more than one guy at a time, this should be stated on the first date. There should be a dating manual that women have to follow because guy's never have any freaking clue what's going on in their relationships until about year three.

You know what sounds like the right thing to do now? Go over and tell her. Yes, that is exactly what I should do! Now, don't get me wrong, I can hear Frank and Claire telling me not to go over, but with their track record of "good" judgement tonight regarding Rick, they are not to be trusted. Yeah, I may have had a few or six beers, but I'm Nathan Smythe and I'm telling you this is the right thing to do.

"Hey Anne, what's up?" I say, trying not to sound at all pissed. I pulled this off flawlessly. Note to self: I need to get my eyes checked because she's a little blurry.

"Hey, Nathan—you ok? You seem mad....? This is Dr. Williams. He is the head of the Education program here at Rollins..." she started to say, but this was banter that was obviously meant to distract me from what was truly going on. I needed to keep my eyes on the prize and not let her beauty take over my judgement.

"Oh, so you have time for this date, but mine has to wait until Friday? You know she's dating me, too, right Doc? It's okay—whatever, Anne. Have a good night. Try and take better care of my sick brother. Good thing he's not dying from a broken heart, because you would suck at that!" At this point I must have been knocking it out of the park because Frank told me that I had said enough. Yeah, I was a verbal destroyer! I didn't need to say another word because I had slayed her date in like, three minutes. I am the master and commander! Although Frank kept apologizing for me, which I'm not sure why because I didn't feel sorry, and Claire said

I would call her tomorrow, which I wasn't going to do; had they not been listening to anything I said to her!? *Are you really my friends or are you servants of Rick?* I told you he was my arch enemy. I bet he hired Professor too-good-looking as well! For some reason they drove my car home, which was fine because obviously that conversation took a lot out of me, and I slept until the next morning.

Chapter 22

heartbreak and hangovers

I think something bad happened last night. I'm not really sure what yet, but I'm feeling like something is a little "off" in my universe. I walked to the kitchen and saw that it was 9:30, which is *way* later than I ever sleep on a Tuesday, or any day for that matter. I also quickly realized that I was supposed to be at work an hour ago and tried to find my phone. It was buried in my pile of clothes, that I don't remember taking off. I found Foxtail on my favorites list and quickly called. Ahmet answered and I explained that I had caught pneumonia overnight and would be back tomorrow. He seemed to buy it.

As I walked into the kitchen I was getting the evil eye from Claire and I needed to know what she did last night that obviously I was upset about.

"How do you feel, dumbass?" she said with more sarcasm than I was ready to hear.

"Why am I a dumbass? You're the one looking all pissed this morning for some reason, what did you do?"

"What did *I do!?* Do you not remember totally abusing Anne in the restaurant in front of her friend?" Claire was now practically screaming, although I don't know why. Wait a minute…

The events of the previous night came flooding back to me as clear as a bell and I found myself feeling a little sheepish, okay, maybe a lot sheepish. God, I am an idiot sometimes. But why wasn't Claire defending me? She has known me for decades, and she just met Anne! She was in the wrong here, Claire!

"I guess I was a little abusive, but why was she out on a date with some other dude? I was pissed."

"Nathan," Claire replied calmly—and sounding more like my mother than I wanted her to. "She is *allowed* to date other people. You guys have only been out *once*. She is *not* committed to you yet. It is *not fair* to put that on her."

She was right, but here's where I differ from the rest of the planet. I already had my next ten years planned out in my head after that first date. I knew that Anne was perfect for me and I was perfect for her, I just needed to get her to see that. This is a part of my psyche that has haunted me forever. I take things way too seriously and I am crushed beyond belief when they don't work out. I needed to relax and let Anne date other guys if that's what it took for her to realize how perfect I am for her. *Yeah, that's probably not going to happen, is it?*

Claire and I talked for about an hour, and I realized what

a major screw up and complete jerk I was. I could never show my face to Anne again. This was a disaster. I had finally found the woman of my dreams and who, for whatever crazy reason had found myself falling in love with, and I had screwed it up, possibly beyond repair.

Marcie walked in (she was still living with us, by the way) and heard the complete and utter fuck up that was her brother. She wasn't judging me like I expected her to do. She just put her hand on mine.

"Nate, you need to talk to her," Marcie calmly said. "Trust me, with the way Joe and my marriage turned out, I wish we had made more of an effort to talk. This is where I failed him, and he failed me. We kept our emotions in check and never thought it was worth it to lay out the problems. We just kept them all hidden for years. And it has finally caught up to us, and I don't know if there is any turning back." She was saying all this and keeping it really together, although I felt like she was verbalizing it out loud to convince herself as much as me. "In these past couple of months, we have made no progress at all, If anything, we are worse off than before, and I don't think it's repairable. We just need to make sure that we are both raising the boys as best as we can. It's about them now, not us. We are done. But we are not done being parents."

Damn. It's just doesn't stop, does it? I mean, I screw up with Anne and now not am I only burdened with that, I am also carrying Marcie's weight as well. I needed to take a walk. A long walk.

Then my phone rang. It was Anne. Crap.

"Hey there," I tried to say with a little smile in my voice.

"Don't 'hey there' me, Nathan. I don't have time for your crap right now. We will talk later. Right now, I need you to go over to Graham's house. He's not feeling well, his nurse needs to leave, and I'm stuck at the garage getting my car worked on after it died last night. Which, by the way, topped off an already shitty night, thanks to your performance! You completely embarrassed me, Nathan. But get over to Graham's and we will discuss this later." And with that she hung up.

Well, I needed some time alone to process all of this, so I didn't tell Marcie where I was going. I just thanked her and Claire for their advice, told them that Anne and I would be talking later, took a shower and drove over to Graham's. At least if he was tired, I wouldn't have to make conversation. I was not in the mood.

I strolled into his house, and his nurse said that she had to run for another emergency but would be returning later this afternoon, she hoped. I needed to watch him because he wasn't sounding good. Great, he better not puke on me. I'd had enough dumped on me already that day.

I found Graham sitting up on his reclining couch. He smiled when I walked into the room.

"You look like shit," he whispered.

"Thanks, you too," I replied.

He patted the seat next to him, asking me to come sit by him. This was not like my brother, as we shared the uncomfortableness of male touching and bonding sometimes. But I sat nonetheless.

"I asked Anne to call you because I needed you here with me today. I don't have any more strength, Nathan. I'm tired. And I'm tired of being tired. I also can't bear to look at Mom or Dad or Marcie today. I just needed my goofball brother here because he won't give me any shit." He paused to catch his breath and continued, "But it's time. I need to be able to go now, and I need you to say it's alright."

No, no, no, no, no…not me. *Not this.* I am not equipped for this. I am not the person put on this planet to handle this. Oh please, let somebody, anybody walk through that door right now. *Oh God, Graham, why?*

I was fighting so hard to hold back the tears, but when he started to cry, I completely lost it. I love my brother. As much of a pompous dumbass as he could be, I love him. And this is not fair. But I also don't want him to hurt anymore either. This was not my Graham. This was a shell of the person I knew, and he wasn't going to get any better. The best I could do was to grant him this peace.

"Of course, it's okay," I said through the tears. I was bawling at this point. There was no turning back now.

"Go." Was all I could muster to say.

And with that, I slid over on the couch and held my brother. I held him like I have never held anyone before. I held him and relived our childhood in my mind. Our adulthood. I didn't hold back the memories or the tears. I cried and cried and so did he. I could feel him sobbing, but after about ten minutes, I could also feel his breathing slowing.

"Thank you," he whispered. And then he stopped. And then he was gone.

I sat and held him for about another fifteen minutes, and then decided I needed to do something. But what exactly is the next step? I've never been with a dead person before. This was uncharted territory for me. Do you Google it? Who do I call? I figured that since Anne was getting paid to handle his affairs, and this plainly fell into "his affairs," she should get the call.

I reached for my phone and found her number.

"What's wrong, Nathan? Please tell me you made it there by now." She was definitely not happy with me today, so I just played it straight.

"He's gone, Anne. About twenty minutes ago. That's why the nurse needed someone."

She was silent, and I hoped I hadn't screwed up so bad that she wouldn't make this worse for me because it pretty much sucked worse than anything else I could imagine. And of course, she didn't.

"I am so sorry, Nathan. I'm driving right now and should be there in about five minutes. Are you okay? Well, I know you're not okay, but, uh, how are you doing? What can I do for you?"

"Nothing at this point," I answered honestly. "Just getting here will be better. I need to call my folks."

I hung up with Anne and made three of the most difficult phone calls I have ever made in my life. My parents, Calvin, and then Marcie, as I saved the worst for last. My Mom took it like a champ, and although she was crying through the phone, she had also come to the mental arrangement that he was not going to get better. I loved this about my mom.

Strength through the storm. She would handle telling Dad, as he was going to be a nutcase like Marcie.

Anne arrived while I was talking to Calvin and started making all the arrangements and calling all the right people. I still, to this day, don't know how she did it, but Graham sure struck gold by hiring her. The coroner showed up and took him out while I was standing right here in the kitchen. So surreal. I was numb at this point and just wanted to leave. Calvin said he would come and get me, and although I knew I eventually needed to be alone, I wanted that right now. I needed to be with my family.

Anne was finally off the phone and had seen the coroner out when Calvin showed up. I'm glad he did, because this was not the time or place for Anne and I to discuss the horrors of last night, and I knew I had a long week coming up. We spoke briefly, and she gave me a hug as Calvin and I left.

On the ride home, we just laughed and cried and really let everything out. It was cathartic, and I could really tell he needed it as much as I did. We made plans to get my car later in the day, and I stumbled into the house.

Claire knew me well enough to know, somehow, that something was not normal. It also took her less than three seconds to piece it together and I saw her start to cry. Ah crap, here we go again. I cried and hugged her for what felt like a long time. The next thing I know Frank is group-hugging and group-crying with us, too. Then Gary joined the party, and all four of us were standing in my living room bawling and holding each other. It was the best part of my day.

I retreated to my room for some much-needed quiet time.

I face-planted on my bed and passed out for about thirty minutes until there was knock on my door.

"Come in," I said groggily.

It was Rick. Really? This is not what I needed at all. I was not about to get into one of our debates, back and forth about the guitar choice of Peter Buck on R.E.M.'s *Monster* album, or why I was such an idiot to Anne, which was none of your business, by the way, Rick!

But instead, "Hey man." Was all that I said. *Typical Nathan.*

"Hey dude, uh Claire called me and told me about your brother and I'm really sorry—that totally sucks. I brought this for you. It helped me when my mom died last year."

And with that, he placed Queen's "Innuendo" album on my bed. For those not familiar with the record, it was the final release by the band in 1991 with lead singer Freddie Mercury. It also contains the haunting, "These Are The Days of Our Lives" track that both captures his frailness in the video, and has some of the most painful lyrics in history, considering how close he was to losing his battle with AIDS at the time. This was a really sweet and thoughtful gesture. I didn't know what to say, but at least this time, I found something not horrible to tell him.

"Thank you, Rick. This really means a lot to me. I actually don't have this one. Thank you."

With that, Rick came over to me and gave me a hug. Oh boy, lots of hugging today. Now, Rick hugging me. Uncomfortable, but yet, really nice. Thank you, Rick.

After he left, I put the record on and blasted it in my headphones for four full listens. While the record overall, is an up-tempo rocker (which reminds me of Graham), it also contains the pain. This is why music is my vice of choice. It not only is getting me to a place mentally that will let me wake up again tomorrow, it has somewhat changed my view of Rick. I mean, maybe what I've been viewing as rivals, have actually been kindred spirits. Maybe what I see as arguments, he views as lively discussions. Maybe he annoys me when I come in to his store because we are both more alike than I thought?

Wow. Too many mental and emotional battles today. This will be a day that I will never forget—and hopefully, will never have to experience anything like it again. But I also sense a change in me. Something new that is starting to bubble up. I don't really have time to deal with it at this point, but after this week is over, I think I need to re-asses my life. Graham may have given me crap for not using my degree more, but he was onto something. I needed to get some ambition going. I was getting stagnant, and I owed it to my brother to do something with my life. I will not let his constant harassing go to waste.

You see that, you big idiot in the sky—I'm finally listening to you!

Chapter 23

candle in the wind

Looking back, the next week went by like a complete blur. We began the funeral arrangements the following day. Mom was trying to be so strong, but I know she was glad to have us around for support. She took care of everything, along with Anne who had most of Graham's financial details, and we all began a week of mourning and remembrance.

We planned the service to be held in Calvin's church, and some of the ladies came together with Marcie and prepared a really nice spread for us. They also cooked meals for my parents that week, which Claire and I brought over and were able to partake in. Graham wanted to be cremated and spread on his property. I'm not sure whose hands that piece of land is going to end up in, but whoever gets it, I hope they are family; otherwise, it's kinda creepy knowing that my dead brother is hanging out in some random person's backyard. I am so glad I had my roommates around this week. It was a much-needed distraction.

Marcie and I arrived at Calvin's church at eight in the morning to make sure that he had everything he needed for the service. There were not many people coming, as Graham was a very busy guy and didn't really have time for friends. My parents got there at 8:30, and while my mom was holding it together the best she could, she was still a mess. Losing a child was something that no one should ever have to go through, and I hated seeing both of my parents this distraught. My dad seemed like he was in another world, and I'm really not sure how much help he was being to Mom, so I stepped in. I sat with her and held her and just let her cry, as this was part of the grieving process she had to go through. She had been strong all week, but the reality of saying goodbye to her oldest child was more than she could take.

People started arriving for the nine o'clock service, and I was pleasantly surprised by how many people Graham's life had touched. He had friends from work, and some others that went to college with him, who had flown in. Claire, Frank, Gary, and Rick came in, and I was very moved by the gesture. I can't believe that I am not repulsed to see Rick here, but my animosity toward him has really diminished since he and I had that musical bonding moment. Marcie found her seat next to me, and she just pressed my hand. No words were needed.

I saw Janine enter at the last minute and sit way in the back. It was obvious that she had been crying, and I'm guessing she didn't want to be noticed. I felt bad for her because it seems that her breakup with Graham had been hard on her. She had put on quite a few pounds, and that does not bode well for her life as a stewardess. (That's her job, by the way. She and Graham had met on an overseas flight and quickly became part of the mile-high club. Typical Graham.) Graham had commented more than once about her "smoking hot body," which was his best compliment for any female, and she had seemed to be letting that go. Poor girl. Marcie had obviously seen her as well as she was now digging her nails into my hand. Ouch! *Settle down, girl!*

"Do you see that!?" Marcie whispered to me, sounding way too excited about Janine's weight gain. Not cool, Marcie—this is Graham's funeral.

"Yeah, I see her, relax. It's not cool picking on her size at a time like this. She obviously gained a little weight after their breakup. Let her be."

Marcie glared at me with the look of *How are you possibly the stupidest person on the planet and how am I even related to you?* I hate when she does that, and she does it way more often than I deserve.

"She's not fat, you moron! She's pregnant!" Marcie scolded.

"Wow, that didn't take long for her to move on. They've only been broken up about four months or so."

"It's more like five, you numbskull, and God you are thick—*it's probably Graham's baby!* How do you survive on a day to day basis?"

Marcie had a point. The really obvious stuff never crosses my mind, and sometimes I'm left feeling like I have the brain capacity of a doorknob. But, *holy crap!* Could this really be Graham's kid? *Why would she come here?* Oh, good gravy, this is going to destroy my mother. She is not strong enough to handle this right now. I need to be the protector.

With that, my mother leaned over to me and said, "Sorry, I didn't tell you about Janine. She's due in June. I guess we'll need to help her along. One thing at a time, right?" And she smiled at me and kissed my cheek.

How the hell is my mother not ruling the world right now? I mean, did I even need to be here? I am beginning to think that she is here for me more than I am here for her. *Unbelievable! My mom knows everything!*

Oh, this is some fresh hell indeed. I glanced over at Claire, and from her expression I could see she knew exactly what I was thinking. How was she ever going to raise this kid and fly all over the world? What a mess. I'm glad Calvin was in his own world talking to what seemed to be a member of his congregation, although somewhat younger. He was getting himself together to perform what was probably one of the most personal and difficult services he ever had to officiate.

With that, the service began, and Calvin was on fire! I have never really heard him preach, but today was a phenomenal and loving message that fluidly wove both stories from Graham's life and scripture passages. He brought most of us to tears, but he was as solid as steel. *What a moving message.* I'm not the most spiritual person, but something was happening in that building.

After the service, we went over to their church hall for a pot luck type of meal. They brought his urn of ashes over, which I found particularly weird, but leave it to Graham to make me feel uncomfortable one more time. Janine stayed and was talking to my mom in the corner. I saw them cry and hug and Janine left without talking to any of the rest of the family.

"Did you have any idea?" Frank asked when we had some time apart from the rest of the group.

"No! He never let on, so I'm not sure he even knew. I mean, all we heard was that they had broken up. With his checkered past, that was not out of the ordinary when it came to Graham's love life. I just figured it was another notch in his belt. When I found out he was sick, I also gave him the benefit of the doubt that he had left her for her own good. You know, so she wouldn't have to see him sick."

Mom came over later and gave Marcie, Calvin, and I the down-low about Janine. She had gotten pregnant back in October, and when Graham broke up with her, she was actually the first one he told about his cancer and swore her to secrecy. She kept her promise, but also kept her own secret. The one where she was carrying his baby. Once she realized how grave his situation was, she made sure that she did not burden him with the news. After he passed last week, she called Mom to tell her. (Not that I think that was the best plan, but I've never been pregnant, so what do I know?) So here we are, in typical Smythe fashion, with a bombshell news delivery taking place at a funeral. Seriously, could my family do anything normal? Why do I feel like Graham is laughing his ass off right now? Not funny, dude! What are we supposed to do with Ms. Pregnant Barbie?

With all this commotion and craziness, I never even found Anne during the whole service. I know she was there, but we never connected. Obviously, we never went on our second date that was supposed to have happened last night, and from what I was told, due to my behavior at The Mill, I may never get the chance. I don't really want to work the sympathy card right now, but if I have to, I am not above it. I finally saw her standing at the back of the hall talking to one of Graham's clients, so I made my way back to her.

"Hey there, thanks for coming," I said, obviously already working the "dead brother" card.

"Of course. I didn't know your brother for very long, but we got pretty close in the time I was able to help him. I'm really going to miss him. I'm glad you were the one he wanted to be with in the end. You were very special to him. He used to tell me all the time how proud he was of you. He said you got all the creative talent in the family, and he always hoped that you could find a way to use it," she replied. Well, *now* who was playing the emotional card? *How was I supposed to respond to that?* That made me feel really, really special. *Damn you, Graham! Now I have to do something with my life!* For Graham, and for this woman standing in front of me. But first, I need to fix all that I have screwed up.

"Well, I owe you an apology," I said. "I'm really sorry how I acted the other night. I saw you on a date with another guy, combined with my having a few too many drinks, and I got stupid jealous, which equals a really stupid Nathan. I don't know what to say, but I hope you forgive me, and I get another chance at a second date."

"Well, first of all, yes, you were really stupid. Secondly, I was not on a date, but you did really embarrass me. That guy I was with is the head of the Education Department at Rollins. He wants to send me to London for a year on an internship to work at a school dedicated to gifted children there. I was working out the details when you made your grand entrance. But yes, I would go out with you again. Maybe after you get through all of this stuff."

Wait a minute. Did I just get great news as well as, quite possibly, the worst news of all time? Yeah, I said that while at the reception following the funeral of my brother. The irony is not lost on me. No, I am not saying her moving is worse than Graham's passing. (Okay, I said it for a minute, but I don't really mean it that way.) I can be kind of melodramatic sometimes. If you hadn't noticed. But, this is *awful*. She wants to go out with me, *then move to London*. You know what kind of people move to London? Really cool people who never come back because they realize how cool they are and how cool it is there, that's who! Not the Nathan Smythe's of the world! No, we do not move to London because there is no way on God's Green Earth we're *that* cool. Ugh! This is a disaster. I do not know how I'm going to navigate this one. But, the first thing I am going to do is accept that second date opportunity, and then start on my devious plan to move there with her. *She will never want me to move there with her.* I imagined punching myself in the face.

"Wow, that is wonderful!" I lied. "I am so sorry I put a damper on that news, but I am so happy for you!" That's two lies in five seconds. "Well, let's get together soon, and you can fill me in on all the details. Can I call you later this week?"

"That would be great." And with that, she kissed me on the cheek. "Have a great week, Nathan. Unfortunately, this means I need to look for a new job, so call me soon before I get busy again."

And with that, she left the reception, and left me standing there in an ocean of emotions that had finally caught up to me. I didn't know how to handle all of this, and I was getting ready to have a major panic attack. Graham's death, Anne leaving, Marcie's divorce, Janine carrying my dead brother's child. It was all too much. I needed to retreat. I sat down on the floor and just tried to breathe. I didn't know if I was going to be able to get through this or not.

I felt someone sit down next to me and rest their head on my shoulder. It was Claire.

"Let's go home," she whispered to me. I just nodded and left without saying goodbye to anyone. I hoped they would understand, but at the moment I didn't really care. I needed some space.

Chapter 24

musical therapy

I don't know if I've mentioned this a hundred times before or not, but music is my world. As a means of escape, as a means of recovery or just as a means of pure enjoyment, music has been my solace for as long as I can remember. I grew up in a very musical household, and I remember attaching a string to an old tennis racket of my dad's to wear as a fake guitar. I was "air guitaring" before it was a thing. One of my first musical memories was coming across an article about John Lennon and his brutal murder. I was sad that such a talented singer was killed by mindless violence. I then pieced together that the Paul McCartney from Wings was also the same Paul in the John, Paul, George and Ringo group. I spent the next few years devouring anything Beatles related and then quickly moved on to any band from the UK.

I understood what my friends who were voracious readers were going through as I was becoming a voracious listener. I would lose myself in my headphones and listen to LPs for hours on end. I would listen intently to hear if I could pick out the bass parts on a certain song, what the vocal harmonies were doing on another, or just imagine the band in the studio recording and creating this magic. It took me to another place where my world was happy.

Today I will be escaping once again, but this time I will be using the playlist from the world of Graham's music. This list will be something similar to a mix-tape he would have had back in the day. It will be some AC/DC, Led Zep, Ozzy/ Black Sabbath, and of course, some Go-Go's (that's one thing we had in common: a love for 80s girl groups). I put these in an order he would have and remember him through the songs.

I listened and could picture him and me through the years. Through his popular-jock high school career, his partying college days, and as we grew up and apart, how are listening choices remained the same. I pictured us in our younger days traveling across the country with our parents, who were always up for a road trip, sitting in the back of the mini-van. Marcie and Calvin struggled with car sickness, so that sent us to "the way back" as we called it. We shared Walkman's and Diet Pepsi's and Doritos. He would have me listen to Ozzy's *Diary of a Madman* and then would school me on the guitar playing genius of Randy Rhoads, while I forced him to listen to Talking Heads *Stop Making Sense*, which, in my opinion, is one of the best live recordings of all time. He never realized how much these times together meant to me. For a short time, I stopped being the annoying little brother and could just be his pal, Nathan. We would laugh at our collective musical nerdiness and end up telling fart jokes.

I'm not even sure how many times I listened through my Graham playlist, but the next thing I knew about three hours had passed. I knew that I needed to come out and talk to my roommates before they called 911. But for a moment I needed to try and piece together how I was going to move forward from all of this. You see, one thing I have not told you was that a few years back I was diagnosed with OCD. I was truly concerned by this at first because I was nothing like the OCD sufferers I saw on TV. I was not overly organized and anal retentive about my clothes or a germ or neat freak. But my struggles with OCD took hold in other ways for me. I have a need for consistency in my life. I like to have a routine, no, let me rephrase that, I *need* to have a routine. I have a strong desire for stability and right now, my family and my world is the opposite of what that is supposed to look like for me. There is not one aspect in my life that looks like it did six months ago. I needed to embrace this new normal, but I also know that, for me, I usually needed to approach something like this with baby steps. But this time that wasn't going to be the case. I was not going to be allowed the benefit of baby steps. I needed to put my big boy pants on and look this new life straight in the eyes. That is terrifying.

And add to that, I have just met the woman who I could possibly spend the rest of my life with. I know, I know, it's only been one date, but you don't understand me, and you probably won't believe me, but I know this is right. I can tell by how we look at each other, the things we talk about, the connection we have made in this short amount of time we have spent together: she is the one. We have been through some really traumatic times and still she wants to spend more time with me. I have been in the dating scene long enough to know what I don't want and what I do want, and I know that I don't want anyone but Anne. I don't know how I'm going to deal with this, but I will figure a way around it. I will woo her for the remaining time we have here, and I will wait for her to come back. Look, it's not like I have a line of women waiting at my doorstep for me. Also, it will give me time to get my life together so that I can be the type of man who is marriage material. I need to focus on a career that doesn't rely on me upselling a muffin with java to pay my rent. I think I will go back and get my teaching certificate and teach music. Yes, I will guide the next generation into a lifetime of musical dedication that only I can provide. It will be perfect, and I will love it! Also, I will not come home smelling like burnt coffee. Hopefully.

Claire and Rick were hanging out in the living room, chatting and listening to Peter Gabriel's first solo album. Great album. Probably one of my top-five favorite songs of all time, maybe even top-three favorite songs of all time. "Solsbury Hill" is the lead track on that record, and I came out just in time to hear it. It instantly calmed my nerves a little.

"Hey mate," Rick said. "You doing okay?"

"Yeah, thanks. I'm feeling much better. Today has really

drained me, though, so I'm probably going to crash early."

"Hey, I think you got a text a bit ago. Your phone was buzzing over there," Claire informed me.

I walked over to the kitchen and saw that I had missed two calls from Anne and a text message.

Just checking on u. Didn't get to say bye to u today. Hope ur ok. Call me.

I had put Anne's shocking news out of my head for a bit while I dealt with my mourning, but I guess this is the first thing I'm going to take on. I unlocked my phone and called her.

"Hey there," she sounded a little tired.

"Hi, sorry I missed your call. I was lying down listening to some music and didn't hear the phone. I was wondering if you wanted to get some dinner tomorrow night?"

"Did you eat today yet? How about dinner right now?"

I was not sure if I was ready to deal with this yet. I mean, I had just gone through my brother's funeral, and I had exhausted myself emotionally for the rest of the day. It was not the best time, mentally, for me to deal with this. But I had really screwed up the last time I saw her and thought I was barely out of the doghouse, probably only because she was feeling a little sad and sorry for me. I should take full advantage of this situation, as I could not have brought her around so quickly on my own.

"Sounds great. Burger Fi near you?" I asked, hoping, as my body needed some grease and starchy carbs.

"Perfect. I'll meet you there in a half hour, cool?"

Well, she doesn't want me to pick her up, so that is not

a great sign, but I agreed and tried to convince myself that even though this was probably not a date and she was heading across the pond soon, this was still going to be a good night.

Chapter 25

back to life

back to reality

Anne and I met at the restaurant. She greeted me with a big hug. It was exactly what I wanted, and I hoped this wasn't just because of the Graham situation, but because she really wanted to see me. It seemed that way, so that's what I'm running with. After we ordered drinks and were perusing the menu, I finally addressed the elephant in the room.

"So, tell me more about this whole England thing. I mean, I just met you and you're changing continents! I know I've scared some girls off before, but they usually just don't return my calls. You've taken it to a whole new level." I was trying to joke to keep myself from freaking out about it. I really did like this girl, and this was a beyond long distance situation.

"Dr. Williams put in for me to intern at this school for the gifted right outside of London. He is getting money together to open a school here in Winter Park based on their philosophy, so he wants me to go there and watch how they do things while he finishes getting the financing together. He figures it will take about a year for that to happen. In the meantime, I can be studying their school. Once that is done, he wants me to help him run the school here. So, I'm only gone for a year, and then, hopefully, come back to my dream job."

"Wow. That does seem perfect. I'm so excited for you, but if I had to be honest, I'm kinda bummed as well. I was really hoping to spend more time with you."

"Well," she smiled. "I was hoping for that too. I don't see why we can't still get to know each other while I'm still here. I don't leave until August, so that gives us about six months to have fun."

I know what my life looked like six months ago, so it scares me to even think what it may be like six months from now. But this was as good an offer as I could have expected given the situation, so I jumped at it. Why wouldn't I want to spend the next six months with a smart, beautiful, funny woman? Even if I get my heart stomped on, it will be worth it. If nothing else, good or bad, I'd have great new playlist material to work with.

We finished our dinner and walked for about an hour around the Rollins campus. I finally told her I was getting really tired from the whole day and I walked her back to her car. I gave her a big hug and we kissed goodnight. I had to get back to work tomorrow, so I told her maybe we could catch a movie Monday or Tuesday. She told me that the play was still happening at the college, so Tuesday night Sherlock was set in stone. *I was not going to screw this one up.*

I drove back to the house and found Marcie sitting up in the living room by herself. I could tell she had been crying. This day was rough on all of us.

"Hey, sis." I called to her as I got myself a beer from the fridge. "Want one?"

"Yes, please. I need it."

"Everything hitting you, too? I was out of it for a few hours in the afternoon just reliving our road trips with Mom and Dad. The ones where you puked, and Graham and I made gross jokes in the back seat."

Marcie forced a smile and finally opened up.

"Yeah, the whole thing is hitting me right now, but I'm actually also pissed at Joe. I mean, he didn't even come to the service. I called him and left a message on his cell. He never answers when he sees that it's me. But he should have come. Graham always treated him really well. Then, I came home to find my divorce papers in the mail. I signed them fast and put them right back in the mailbox. Then it just kinda hit me. My marriage is over. I'm a failure at being a wife and not much better at being a mom. I could never be the mom Mom is. She just has her shit so together. I just wanted to make them proud. And I can't. I just can't."

She was bawling by this point, and I know she didn't want this to be about her, but I'm not the best at making folks feel better, but I was turning over new leaves, right? Maybe I could try and actually be a little sensitive right now. I'm going to give her my deepest and most soulful attempt at being the loving brother. Here we go, I can do this.

"Yeah, that sucks."

Wow. Maybe I'm not so good at this. Okay, what would Calvin say? No, I can't pull that off. Ah hell, let me try this again.

"You're not a failure. From what I'm told, marriage is two people working at it, not one. So, you both failed." Damn it, Smythe, is it possible to say anything that doesn't sound like you just removed your head from your behind?

"What I'm trying to say is, even though you and Joe weren't meant to be, doesn't mean you're a failure. You tried and it didn't work out. Your kids are still young, and you have plenty of time to be a good mom. Just because you've sucked at it so far, doesn't mean you can't make it right."

I smiled and rubbed her shoulder. Then I handed her a beer and realized that was probably the most help I'd given her in the past five minutes.

"Thanks, Nathan. In your backwards and stupid way of saying things, you actually made me feel a little better. I don't have to dwell on my failures, I can move on from them and be better in the future." She looked like she honestly believed it.

See, I can give support! Nobody needs to know how many times I screwed it up, just as long as, at the end of the day, I made her feel a little better.

We sat up for a few more hours talking about our childhood and Graham and how we were going to take care of Janine and this baby that we didn't even know existed. We knew we needed to come up with a plan, but we had no idea what that was going to be at this point. I figured I could get her number from Mom and maybe Marcie or Calvin could call her.

You didn't really think I was going to call her, did you? You did just hear how bad the conversation just went with my own sister, right? There is no way I'm going to attempt to talk to an almost complete stranger about how she is going to handle her pregnancy. No way, no how. I am NOT calling Janine.

So, the next day I called Janine and decided that maybe we could meet for a drink later in the week. She informed me that pregnant women don't drink. I thought to myself, *uh, yeah you do, that's probably how you got pregnant*, and then I realized she meant *after* the sex part, so I'm glad I didn't say that out loud. We agreed on coffee. Decaf. (I guess pregnant women don't drink that either.) We'll be meeting at Foxtail after I get off work one day this week.

Chapter 26

papa don't preach

I got ready for work the next morning and I mentioned to Frank that I was meeting Janine later that day. (She had texted me back last night to see if I was available.)

"What are you guys going to do about the baby? Are you guys planning on taking care of it?" Frank wondered.

"I have no idea yet. All I know is that I am meeting her, and I'm going to try and figure something out. I mean, my parents can't do it, Marcie and I are out of the question, and I don't think Calvin is in the market for a family yet."

Frank laughed and said, "No, I don't think so. After all, he is just getting a little braver with being in public with Paul and all."

"I don't know if he's public or not yet. I mean, I don't know how much they have been seen together yet."

"What are you talking about? Didn't he introduce you to him at Graham's ceremony? Who did you think Calvin was talking to in the back of the church before he gave the eulogy? I mean, they were holding hands, Nathan!"

"Really? I saw that guy, but just assumed it was someone from Calvin's church. I didn't even notice them holding hands."

"Someone from his church? Nathan, there hasn't been a member of that church under seventy for the past two decades. Sometimes, I wonder about you, dude."

So, there you have it. I am officially the most clueless person on the planet when it comes to affairs of my family. I'm sure Mom already met Paul, and Marcie probably has his contact info in her phone and on her Christmas card list for next year. *Sometimes my life exhausts me.*

I pull into work hoping for some relief from the stress that comes with being in the Smythe clan, and I see that I am alone with Jessica today. Well, that can be good or bad, depending on her recent escapades with the male persuasion, so let's see how today goes.

"Hey, man," she greets me. "I heard about your brother. Sorry, man, that really sucks. Cancer's a bitch."

"Yeah, it is—thanks, Jess" I walk in and start making drinks right away as there is a line already, and I hear that she has The Housemartins 1986 album *London 0 Hull 4* playing, and I am instantly in a better mood. Nothing lifts your spirits like a little 80s British Alternative tuneage. When I hear these records again, it's what I imagine running into a long-lost friend you haven't seen forever would be like while catching up on all the news of the past twenty years. It sounds completely dreadful to have to do that with another human, but an LP, that's pure joy.

We spend most of the day making small talk, then I fill her in on the drama of the Janine baby.

"Holy crap, are you kidding me!? That's like right out of a rom-com flick. That shit never happens in real life! Only to you, Smythe." She is intrigued and obviously curious about how this is all going to pan out. The problem is, I have no idea just yet.

"If she's still carrying that kid, she must want it a little, right?" she continues. "I mean, who would do that and just walk away? She must be hoping one of you guys will take it."

That is exactly what I'm afraid of. Tomorrow we are meeting with the lawyers to go over Graham's estate, and maybe we will get more of a clue there as I was told by Marcie that Janine is expected to be there. I know that she and Graham got along better than most of his girls, but I am kinda surprised to hear that she is part of his will. I'm also surprised that I am in a family of someone who has enough of an estate to require a lawyer's meeting. *What is this, Downton Abbey?*

I finish my shift, and I see that Janine has arrived for our little meeting. To be honest, I had actually forgotten I was meeting her, so it's a good thing she ordered some coffee.

We sit down, and I can tell she is already feeling a little defensive. So, I decide to break the ice a little.

"So, how are you feeling?" I ask as politely as possible.

"I'm pregnant, Nathan. How do you think I feel? I'm fat

and tired and uncomfortable everywhere I go. I can't eat anything yet, but I'm always hungry. I feel nauseous and fart a lot, so about as unsexy as I could possibly be. And the father of my child died last week. So, yeah, not so great."

The sarcasm wasn't necessary, but I got where she was coming from. She was hurting, and her pain was being misdirected at me. In case she wasn't sure, I lost my brother last week, too. But this wasn't about me, or her, it was about the baby, and I needed to know where her head was before tomorrow.

"So, I know you are going to be at the meeting tomorrow, and I'm wondering what you are thinking about once the baby is born? Are you going to raise it here? Are you going to keep traveling? I'm not trying to be nosy, but it is my niece or nephew, and with my brother gone and all. I really do just want to help. I know my mom is concerned as well, but she can't handle thinking about this right now." I tried not to sound too accusatory or pushy, but this talking to a stranger thing (I've only met her twice) was not my strong suit.

She softened a little, and I could tell that she believed me and was willing to at least have a conversation.

"I'm going to keep traveling, but I don't think I'm going to be able to keep the baby. I have never wanted to terminate the pregnancy, but I am looking for a loving couple who wants a child. There are agencies I can join, or I can choose to do it on my own through a lawyer and stuff. I hope you and your family understand because once that decision is made, you may not be able to visit or see the child at all, depending on the new parents. I hope you can explain this to your folks. I'm sorry."

It was heartbreaking to hear and to think about never getting to know Graham's child, but this was her call. It was her body and her baby. I was not going to stand in her way. I would just help out where I could. We drank our coffees and made some small talk and left the café about an hour later. I told her I would see her in the morning and gave her my number in case she ever needed to call me.

I decided to head home and crash early. I knew tomorrow was going to be stressful, so I needed to get some shut-eye. I filled Claire, Frank, and Gary in on my conversation with Janine. I then texted Anne and told her that I'd call her after Graham's meeting, and she suggested we grab some dinner tomorrow night. I love that idea, and sleep, really well.

The next morning, I pulled out my "big boy" suit and headed to the lawyer's office. It is located out by Graham's old house in Dr. Phillips area and there is more money in the car collection in his parking lot than I will probably ever see in my lifetime.

We all met in the big main conference room, and I could see that Mom was struggling. She knew this was the final stop on her journey with her oldest child, and it was incredibly heartbreaking. My dad wasn't fairing much better, but Mom showed it in her eyes. Her zest for life was nonexistent. Marcie and Calvin sat across from me, and Janine sat next to me just staring at the floor. The lawyer finally arrived. Apparently, having decided that we'd all been sitting in awkward silence for long enough.

"Good morning, everyone, my name is James Anderson,

and I am the executor of Mr. Graham Smythe's estate. I will hereby break it down as easily as possible as there is quite a bit to dole out, but it is pretty straightforward."

Quite a bit to dole out? I mean, I knew Graham had some cash, but was never really sure exactly how much.

"Mr. Smythe was worth about twenty-five million dollars and had most of that tied up in assets and investments, which he has put into a trust-fund for Miss Cashman's unborn baby to be awarded in installments throughout the child's life. He also had a cash amount of just over five million dollars that he has spilt between his family members. Two million dollars is awarded to his parents Mr. and Mrs. James Smythe. One million dollars is awarded to each of his siblings, Rev. Calvin Smythe, Mr. Nathan Smythe, and Mrs. Marcie Donovan. His property is awarded to his unborn child and the child's family, which I assume will be you, Miss Cashman?"

Holy crap! You could see the look in her face. This whole time Janine was wondering why she was here at all *and wham!* Fresh from the grave, Graham hits a doozy of his own. He knew she was pregnant and never let on! *My family is getting more and more freaking bizarre by the day!*

"Ummm, no," she stuttered, clearly taken aback by all of this and was starting to get overwhelmed. "I..uh...I'm giving the baby up, but I don't know to whom yet, so I guess whoever that ends up being will get the house."

Well, crap. I never got to tell my family that she was giving the baby up, and my mom did not look pleased. But she also knew this was not her choice and that she needed to keep the peace for Graham's memory. Oh, and by the way—I just made a million bucks! What!? Ho-ly Shit!! First thing I'm doing is buying a new turntable. And maybe a ticket to London. *For the whole year.*

"Yes, that is exactly what will happen," Mr. Lawyer-man continued, "as soon as you know who the family is going to be, please get in contact with my office and we will make all the legal arrangements. If there are no questions, we are finished here."

He started to get up and Calvin interrupted him.

"Actually, yes, I do have a question. Being that Miss Cashman was basically left out of the will and is carrying my brother's baby, I would like to donate a quarter of my inheritance to the family that adopts the baby."

"I would like to do the same as well," Marcie chimed in.

"Us, too," my dad whispered.

Ah, hell. I'm a millionaire for ten minutes and everybody has to open their big mouths. *Seriously?* Couldn't we buy the kid a gift card or something? Uggghhhh. Sometimes I hate these people and all their utter goodiness.

"Yeah, same here." I smiled. *Sometimes I'm a good liar.*

Janine began to cry, and I knew that deep (way deep) in my heart this was the right thing to do.

As we exited the conference room, we were greeted by Frank, Claire, and Gary. *What were they doing here?* Did they hear of my windfall already and want to pillage my earning like vultures? How dare they, I could see it in their eyes, they had no good intentions here.

"Janine!" Frank called as he and Gary ran up to her.

"Nathan told us last night that you are looking for families to adopt your baby and we want to be that family! We know that we have to move up the wedding but we'll totally do that and let you have full visitation if you want. We have always talked about having a family and what a better way than to have one of my best friend's niece or nephew."

Janine was now full on bawling. "I would love that!" She was so happy and excited about this possibility. Mom started crying and Dad was beaming from ear to ear. I walked up to both Frank and Gary and gave them both really huge hugs. *This was amazing!* And Frank didn't even know yet that they had just inherited Castle Smythe and a million dollars!

Chapter 27

london calling (not)

I spent the rest of the day with my family and barely had enough time to get home, change, and make it to the restaurant to meet Anne. I was on cloud nine, I mean, really, seven hundred and fifty thousand dollars! It was more than generous, and the only sad thing is that I'm not able to thank Graham in person. I hope that he is somewhere where he knows how happy and appreciative I am. But I would rather have my brother back, trust me.

I arrived at the restaurant and Anne already had a table waiting for us. I started in on the whole week telling her first about my conversation with Janine, then the meeting with Graham's lawyer, and then the total whammy of Frank and Gary adopting Graham's baby. My head was completely buzzing, and now I was looking at her beautiful face, this night could not get any better.

"Nathan, I think we need to stop seeing each other."

And with those ten words, my heart crumbled. I had been on this end of the conversation way too many times, but I had no idea why I was there right now. *What did I do?* I mean, I thought I apologized for my night of shame at The Mill?

"What the hell happened? What's going on? Just a couple of days ago you thought this was a good thing?"

"This is a *great* thing and that's the problem. I've looked at my plans for the fall and I have a lot of work to do. I can't get distracted by anything right now. This is what I've worked for all these years. I want this more than anything, and the problem is, you are a distraction. Actually, the real problem is, I really, really like you. Way more than I thought I was going to. But I don't ever want to regret you, Nathan. I don't ever want to worry that you stopped me from reaching my goals. I'm really sorry. If this was happening in almost any other way, we could work it out. But I am leaving for London for a year. That is a long time. I don't know what life will look like when I get back, but I know that I need to have space right now. I'm sorry."

And with that, she got up, kissed me on the cheek, and walked out of my life. I just sat there. For a really long time. Finally, I left the restaurant and just walked. And walked. And walked. This person was supposed to be my soul mate. We had such a connection, I can't even begin to explain it. I was crushed. She was going to find someone else. This wasn't going to turn out okay for me. This is always how it happens. I don't even know what I do wrong or how I push people away. I mean, I do know I do it. I'm arrogant and insecure all at the same time. I'm an introvert and someone who runs his mouth. I don't let you get close. *But I let her.* She was not just let into my world, she was let *way* in. *What was I going to do now?* I didn't want to go home, but I didn't want to be alone either. I called Marcie and asked if she could meet me at Will's Pub. At least I could commiserate with someone else who just screwed up their relationship.

I was already a couple of beers in when Marcie arrived. She knew by looking at me that something was wrong, and it didn't take a rocket scientist to figure out what it was. We sat there and traded heartbreak stories and both of us got mad and sad and frustrated together. Finally, she asked the question I didn't want to hear.

"So, what are you going to do now?" Brilliant Marcie. Just brilliant.

"Well, actually, I'm going to get my teaching certificate and teach music. I'm done with the slacker job thing, and I think it's time I made Graham proud and started to actually use my degree like he always wanted me to. I think I'm also going to write a book about the history of 80s indie/alternative music, just because I can. But first I'm going to teach. I need to have a purpose in my life, and right now, Anne has sucked the life out of me. I need to get it back."

"Well, personally, that sounds like a shitty plan because those kids are going to drive you nuts, but I support whatever you want to do." Marcie was getting drunk and her honesty was bubbling to the surface. It's okay, they probably *will* drive me nuts, but I can take it, I think.

We ordered some food so we could get sober and I

followed her back to my place. My playlist pulled up Elvis Costello and I just wallowed in some "Every Day I Write The Book" and other classics that set my mood to blue. It will be okay. I can get through this. But if I do, and I don't suffer from a major nervous breakdown, it will be nothing but a miracle.

We got home and Claire, Rick, Frank, and Gary were still up and busting at the seams with excitement. This is what I needed after a night like tonight. I'm not even going to broach the subject of Anne. I just want to soak in some wedding and adoption plans right now. It was decided that the whole ceremony, reception, and after party were going to take place at Graham's, or now, Frank's place. They are going to invite only about one hundred people, so the party will be reasonable. Gary's mom had a change of heart (his dad had not), but his mom will be coming after all. She will be giving her son away, and that is making him so proud. It had taken a lot for this to happen, and I feel like it is all falling into place for them. I asked Frank about the playlist and was told that Rick was going to DJ the event, so I'd need to confer with him. I paused, took a deep breath, and realized that I was actually not mad at all about that. I thought Rick was going to make a great DJ and I looked forward to his music choices. I'd even go so far as to tell him this. I hope he realizes the immensity of that gesture. But, he doesn't.

It's never a good sign when there is someone pounding on your door at three in the morning. I could hear that it was Clair, and I really didn't need her drunken mumbling at this point.

"Clair go to bed!" I shouted hoping to shake her back to sobriety.

"Nathan, get your ass out of bed, it's Marcie. I think she's having a heart attack!"

What the hell is happening to my siblings?? I rushed out of my room to find Marcie in the fetal position, shaking and sweating.

"My chest is killing me and I haven't slept for the past few nights. I'm sorry, Nathan."

She was sobbing and rocking and I'm no Einstein, but I knew this wasn't good. I got down on the floor next other and just held her for awhile. When the pain didn't go away, we were able to convince her to go with us to Florida Hospital down the road. One look at her and she was admitted right away. These nurses weren't screwing around for whatever reason and they took her back for about two hours.

Finally a doctor came out and tried to calm us down.

"Your sister has had a nervous breakdown. We will need to keep her for observation for a few days. She has raised some concerns about harming herself and we need to keep her. I'm sure you understand."

We filled out all the pertinent paperwork and I put myself down as her next of kin. Kind of weird as Joe has always been their for her, but I Couldn't even reach him by phone. When he finally texted me back all he said was, "Let me know how she is" Dick. Don't you even want to see the mother of your children? Bastard. Whatever, I'm here for her now and I will do all I can to take care of her.

She stayed in the hospital for two week and in that time,

I did as much research as I could on people with severe depression and asshole husbands. Surprisingly, they seem to go hand in hand. Nevertheless, I am going to be here for her and I will be her rock. I've never been anyone's rock before, so yeah, this oughta be interesting.

Chapter 28

with or without you and me

The next two months were a blur as we prepared for both an upcoming wedding and the birth of our nephew. (Yes, she found out the gender.) I'm not sure if that makes Frank and I some kind of weird brother-in-law relationship? I kept moving forward without trying let my mind wander off to Anne too often. But that was not easy. I would swear I saw her when I went to the grocery store. Or Target. Or in the car next to me. But it was never her. And when she ended it, she really ended it. I mean, I texted her once in a while and I would get a one-or-two-word answer. Nothing more. I was devastated and tried my best to work through it. But I'm still holding out hope.

I built my post-Anne playlist the day after she broke up with me. It consisted of some of the best break up songs of all time:

There Is A Light That Never Goes Out, The Smiths

The Break-up Song, The Greg Kihn Band

Every Breath You Take, The Police (A very creepy song if you really read the lyrics.)

But you get the idea. Woe is me. I spent more time at Rock n Roll Heaven, as Rick and I were friendlier than we had ever been, and Claire was now a pretty serious thing in his life. *How did that relationship work out? What the hell, Rick?* I have to stop. I can't hate Rick because Anne chose to be responsible about not dating me. I mean, what she said and did makes sense, I just hate it. I also made sure that I was there whenever Marcie needed me without making her feel like she was an emotional invalid.

We all began our different roles to get ready for the upcoming celebration. Marcie was putting together one of the most delicious all-vegetarian menus I had ever seen. I mean, I am a true carnivore, but if she was cooking for me, I think I could handle a plant-based diet. It was full of fresh fruit, rice dishes, and some exotic veggie plates that she was borrowing from Ahmed from Foxtail. His family was from Pakistan and ate a mostly vegetarian diet, so they had some delicious recipes as well. Marcie and I were meeting that morning to do some pricing and shopping because I had the day off and the wedding was a week away.

As she walked into the kitchen, I could see this was not going to be a good day; something was definitely bothering her. I really wanted to avoid the conversation, but I was alone in the house with her, so there was no one else to pass this off to, and she obviously needed to talk. *Why can't I just walk up to someone in need and just hug them? No words. Just hugs.* My life would have been so much easier this past year, but here goes.

"Hey, what's up? You don't look like you're in great spirits today. Something bugging you?"

With that, the tears started, and I was caught again in emotional turmoil. Oh, good Lord…

"Joe has decided to marry the woman he was having an affair with. And they're moving. To St. Louis. That's where *her* family is from. He's taking the boys. And as I much as I want to fight it, I know that this is the better option for them. I mean, I'm a mess, just working as a freelance caterer for Frank. Up there, they have her family and cousins that are their age. It's killing me inside that being away from me is the best thing for my kids! He's such an asshole! I hate him, Nathan. I hate him with every fiber of my being. My life has been ruined by this bitch, and now I will have to live without my children. I won't be around for their first relationships. I won't be there when they come home after playing their first soccer game. Or their first dance. Or learn how to drive. I hate this, Nathan."

She continued to cry and cry, so I held her. Maybe I was going to luck out this time and not have to have any dialogue; she really didn't need to hear anything from me. She just needed to vomit her anger about Joe. But I had to agree with her, this was a dick move. If he wanted to get married and be with his new slut, he could, at least, have done it locally. But all I could do was try and distract Marcie from her own crap. So, grocery shopping we will go. Boy, aren't we a pair? Two love-lost souls, wandering around Whole Foods looking for deals on avocados for dip. So poetic.

When we got back from the store, Marcie put some of the food that could be purchased early away to prepare for Saturday. Being that it was Monday, and I was off today, I decided that since I had committed to teaching music next year, I needed to start studying for the test and take it soon. I cracked open the book and quickly realized how much I had forgotten in the years since college. This was going to be a long road. And then something hit me. Did I really want to teach little kids how to play the recorder? Not really. I wanted to teach the history of music. Mostly rock music, but I could handle a little Mozart as well. I had been granted the benefit of not needing to work for a while, thanks to Graham. *Maybe I should go back to school and get a Master's degree in Music History and teach that instead?* While that would both delay having to study, it also allowed me to focus on something else besides Anne. Because, no matter what I tried to do, my heart still hurt from losing her. I would take this studying thing more seriously if I enrolled and had some accountability, so that became my plan. I decided to head over to UCF the next day. It was also time to put in my notice at Foxtail. Since I had already taken the week off for Frank and Gary's wedding, it seemed like the perfect time.

We have our tux fittings scheduled, so I stopped by Foxtail on the way.

"Hey, Ahmed," I greeted him as I walked in. The store was pretty quiet. Bert was working the bar, and Ahmed was putting up some new hipster-style décor that his wife probably picked out. She had a brilliant eye for aesthetics, and whatever she chose usually worked out great.

"So, what do you think? Does this look urban-rustic-upcycled enough? I have no decorating ability at all. Pyria is coming by later, and I promised her it would be done by now. I've had the new decorations for a month and haven't put them up yet." He laughed.

I just smiled. Typical Ahmed. I would miss working for him. He's a great guy, but it was my time to move on. I told him about my plan, and he smiled and gave me a hug, telling me he was happy for me and that he had been worried about me, with all my family has gone through this year. I thanked him for all the years I had been there and promised to visit often, as I would be needing lots of java to get through my studies. I told Bert real quick as I was leaving, and I was surprised how sad he was to hear it. We're not that close, but you never realize the bonds you make with people when you see them day in and day out and battle the world of coffee-snobs together. I made a mental note that I needed to stop by and see Jessica before the week was out.

I made it to the tux shop at 4:15 and realized I was fifteen minutes late. Frank, Gary, Calvin, and who I assume was Paul were waiting for me. I walked in and greeted everyone.

"Hey, guys—sorry I'm late," I said.

"No biggie," replied Gary as his phone went off and he left to take the call.

Calvin then walked over to me and finally made the intro.

"Nathan, this is Paul. We have been dating for a few months now. Sorry it's took so long to introduce you two, but we've been keeping it a little quiet. I know that I have gone public, but being in a relationship is something I'm going to ease into with my congregation. We have to keep a low profile right now. We've been out with Frank and Gary a few times, because Paul and Gary actually knew each other through a mutual friend. Small world, huh?" Calvin could certainly see the irony in that. He and Frank swam in similar circles as well, unbeknownst to both of us.

"Well, it's good to meet you," I said and shook his hand. I'm sorry you're dating my brother as he is kind of a pain in the ass, but best of luck to you." I smiled at Calvin as he rolled his eyes. Paul seemed like a good enough guy and I was truly happy for him. I brought him up to speed on Marcie and told him that maybe she could use some of his guidance at a time like this, and honestly, I really didn't want her crying on me again.

Gary walked in, and Frank instantly saw something was wrong with his partner.

"What's wrong, Gar?" he asked.

Gary was trying his best to control himself, but he was really, really angry.

"That was my mother. She is *not* coming after all. She thought she was okay with us, but she has been really thinking about it lately and she cannot condone this marriage. She lives in a world where this is not accepted in her social circle of snobs. I can't stand her sometimes. I have battled this ever since I told her, but I think that I have reached my limit. I am cutting her out of my life. I can't continue to go back and forth with her anymore. I'm sorry, Frank. I love you, but it seems my family doesn't share that love."

He was crushed. He had been picturing his mother walking him down the aisle and giving him away for weeks. It was only days before the event, and she pulls this?

"I'll give you away," said Paul. "I would be honored and certainly don't mind."

"That would be wonderful," said Gary. "I really don't want to walk down the aisle alone. It sucks enough that I basically have no family here. I don't want to feel like a loser who can't even get someone to support him on the most important day of his life."

So, it was settled, Paul would give away Gary and I would give away Frank, and Calvin would bond them together. It was going to be beautiful. I was a little jealous of Frank actually.

Chapter 29

nice day for a ~~frank~~ wedding

So, the day finally arrived. I got to Graham's house at nine to get ready for the ten o'clock wedding. Being that it was a brunch-like affair, Marcie had created some breakfast and lunch-type goodies. She had done an amazing job with both the preparing and presentation of the event. She was looking better today as well, as she had come to terms a bit with the way her life was moving. She was not happy about it, but she was going to soldier on. She was going to make sure that she visited her boys when she could, but she also realized that she had to pick up the pieces of her own life and not let herself wallow in self-pity forever. She was going to be okay, but it wasn't going to be easy.

I had spent the past two days on the campus of UCF and met with multiple advisors to begin my future endeavor.

I was going to have a lot to study, and I was definitely going to take my time and do it right. It was exhausting to think about, so I was happy to have the wedding to focus on instead. There would be no other distractions in my life during the wedding! *Whew.*

Then Anne walked in. She looked gorgeous. What was *she* doing here? *Why would Frank do this to me?*

"Why did you invite Anne?" I questioned. I could see that was exactly what he wanted to talk about. Sarcasm. He was in no mood for my shenanigans, and I really couldn't blame him, but I don't care, I wanted answers.

"Your brother gave us this place to have our ceremony and to raise his...our upcoming child. The least I could do was invite the caregiver who was with him until the end." Frank replied gruffly.

"No, actually, the *least* you could have done was nothing, which would have included *not* inviting her. And by the way, I was with him at the end, not her! She was busy being mad at me." I reminded him. But that was the end of talking about it. I composed myself and decided that wasn't the day to upset Frank, and I would be the bigger person.

The ceremony began and went flawlessly. Paul was effortless in his role, and Calvin's sermon and overall performance was great. They both looked so happy, and Gary didn't seem like he was thinking or worrying about his family at all. He was enjoying the moment and beginning the rest of his life. Rick played the part of wedding DJ with such class, I had to tell him that I was impressed. His combination of traditional wedding music with some classical pieces followed by tasteful pop music, not from this decade, couldn't be beat. Even by me.

I kept stealing glances at Anne. I wasn't really mad that she was at the wedding, it was just that it kept bringing my emotions to the surface. I was trying to keep my stuff together, but there she was. In all her perfection. I needed to figure out a way to make this work. C'mon, Smythe! Get your head together and win this girl! You need her to make your life whole. She knows that as well, that is why she is afraid. She wants this to work out, but she can't figure out a way to make it happen, so she ended it. Are you going to remain on the sideline of life forever, Nathan, or are you going to get in the game? Not that I usually responded well to sports analogies, but for some reason this seemed appropriate in my head.

We finished the service and started the food round, and I made my way over to her. It was like the first time I had asked her out all over again. I was nervous and sweating and hoping to God that I wasn't starting to stink. Nothing says "I'm your smooth and suave future husband" like pit stains and b.o.

"Hey there," I said as I moved next to her in the guacamole line. *Great opening line, Romeo.*

"Hi. How have you been? You look nice, by the way. Good job up there. I was sure you were going to forget the rings." She laughed and teased me.

"You look phenomenal as well. If I can be honest, I've been staring at you all day wondering what I was going to say to you. You still make me nervous as heck, you know." I wasn't lying either. I had no clue how this conversation was going to go, but I knew that it had to happen.

"You're too sweet. I've missed you. I've missed us. But I'm still so scared about going away. And I'm sorry if I hurt you, Nathan, but I didn't really know what else to do." She looked like she had been thinking about this, too. Like maybe she had been as torn over me as I had been over her. So, without hesitation, I just said it.

"Anne. I have to be honest with you. I know we only saw each other a couple of times, but we did spend a lot of time together with Graham. And, I can honestly say, I have never felt like this before. I have never been so distraught about losing someone as I have been about you. So here it is, I think I love you."

"Nathan, please stop."

Anne interrupted what was probably going to be my best speech ever. *This can't be good.*

"I can't think about this right now," she continued. "I have to leave for London soon, you just lost your brother, and I honestly can't handle talking about it. I'm only going away for a year, and, quite honestly, as much as I might want to, I can't ask you to drop everything in your life and follow me. I won't be *that* girl. And I wouldn't let you do it anyway. You'd just end up resenting me. If we can just stay in touch and see how things are when I get back, that would be great. I really care about you, but just thinking about starting up this whole mess again stresses me out."

Well then, that went just about as shitty as it possibly could have. How could she not see the depth of sacrifice I'd be willing to make for her? I am the man of her dreams, she just doesn't see it yet. *How will I wait for a year?* I mean, really, Anne, *a whole year?* I needed to say my piece before she walked out. I needed to *not* be my normal Nathan self, living inside my head. But then she kissed me on the cheek, gave me an almost uncomfortably long hug, and said the second most heartbreaking thing I'd heard recently. "Goodbye, Nathan. Please take care of yourself and stay in touch. I promise we can revisit this when I get back. I really do care about you." And with that, she stabbed me in the heart and walked out. Out of my life and soon to be out of the country. She might as well have been going to the Space Station for as much as I would be able to see her.

When we were done embracing, I saw Claire staring at me. She gave me the dorkiest thumbs up ever. No, Clair, that was not a thumbs-up moment. That was not at all how I was hoping today was going to end. I'm not really sure how I thought Frank's wedding was supposed to affect me, but I am always the center of my own attention. I mean, I didn't even know she was coming and then, somehow, I turned that into a complete cluster. Well, I did need to get my shit together. I needed to be there for Marcie, and for Frank and Gary. I also needed to be there for Janine and the birth of Alexander Graham—yeah, like the telephone guy, but it was a fitting tribute for my brother. *Maybe it wasn't time for Anne and I to begin our journey together.* Either way, a year away from Anne was too long. I looked around at all the happy people gathered for the wonderful event and decided I'd be damned if my stupid crap was going to put a dent in Frank's day. He deserved better. I only wished that my parents had been able to make the wedding, but I just don't think Mom was ready to be in Graham's house just yet.

I spent the next couple of hours mingling and trying to wrap my head around what had transpired. There are times in your life when you just have to do what you need to do, even when it goes against everything that other folks think is right. And against most people's better judgment, this was one of those times. I sat down with Marcie as the night was winding down and we shared a couple of whiskeys.

"You did an amazing job today," I told her. "I really never doubted you, but to actually see it come together. You are really great. I don't know if you noticed Anne and I talking before. But it was good to see her again."

"Yeah, she looked great. I hope you were nice to her; you tend to be an idiot when you're not really sure how to act."

Marcie has a way of combining an insult and a piece of advice better than anyone I'd ever known. You always left not quite sure whether she had just insulted you or helped you out. Or maybe both.

"Yeah, I was civil. You know she leaves in a couple of weeks. She's going to be gone for a whole year and we just started to really get to know each other. I'm thinking about doing something really crazy, Marcie. I think I'm going to follow her to London. I think I'm going to surprise her."

If there was anyone in the world right now who would understand and agree with me, it was Marcie. I mean, she was going through her own stuff, but no one on the planet was as up for a big change and taking risks as my sister.

"Are you out of your fucking mind! Who on God's Green Earth would do something like that!? You're a freaking nut job, Nathan. Please don't do that! She will hate you for it. No one wants someone else butting in on their big life choices. She is going away to start something new and the last things she needs is for you to be interloping on her new life."

Thanks, Marcie. *Maybe I should stop talking to women today as they seem to be my Kryptonite.*

"Marcie, this isn't about me going over there to ruin anything. This is about me going over there to find something. I have spent my life floating in and out of relationships only finding solace in my music. Now, I finally find someone who not only connects with me romantically but emotionally as well, and I'll be damned if I'm going to let her get away. Trust me, as much as most people think I'm an idiot, I have actually spent the past few days thinking about this quite seriously. Which, for me, is an eternity. I will go over there and see how things go. Yes, it will be a surprise; yes, there will be some drama. But, if we are meant to be, then I am making the right choice. Waiting for a year will drive me absolutely nuts, and I'm in a situation right now where I can afford to do this. Please support me. You are one of the only people right now who is going through their own relationship crap. I know I'm nuts, but hearing you lie to me and tell me I'm going to be okay is actually what I need."

She smiled, and for the first time in quite some time, I felt like she got me.

"Okay, if that's what you really need to do, then do it. I will be here when it goes to shit, but you are right. Sometimes you just need to take that chance. I mean, *what the hell do you have to lose?* I think I've decided something as well. I'm using some of the money Graham left me to hire a custody lawyer to ensure the kids spend summers with me, and I'm going to open a bakery and catering service. I've always wanted to be in business for myself, and College Park could use a new bakery. Maybe I could get Ahmed to sell some of his coffee there and we could kind of partner together."

"That's brilliant, Marcie. When I get back from the UK, I can always help out at the bakery, and with the kids if you need it. God knows I have enough barista experience. I can work on getting better at the babysitting thing. Or maybe I'll just take the kids over to Calvin's, then come in and eat and leave the barista-ing and baking to you." I laughed and held her hand.

"Thank you for everything, Nathan. You have been more than just a brother to me these past few months. You've kept Calvin and I strong through Graham's death, you've given me a place to live, and way more than once you've been a shoulder for me to cry on. You've really become my best friend, you know. I'm going to miss you. Anne is perfect, and more than that, she is perfect for *you*. You guys are going to be great."

I knew she was right. We *were* going to be great. Actually, we were going to be better than great. We were going to be perfect. I need to make a playlist about this. About how two people come together and make a new life together attacking the unknown. You don't see that too much anymore. There's too much heartbreak and too much lying in relationships nowadays. Too many kids are not seeing good examples of love. But I think Frank and Gary will be great. I think Claire and Rick will be okay. And I know that Anne and I will be forever. Forever people in a not-so-forever world. A couple of not-so-common people.

Acknowledgements

I would like to thank:

My wife, Melissa, for being my beta reader, conscience for Nathan, and loving and supporting me when I thought this book was just a dumb idea.

Vanessa Anderson and Indie Owl Press for taking a chance on me and feeding me with great insight, direction, and confidence.

Morrissey and Marr for a lifetime of musical inspiration.

T Gamache was born and raised in Rhode Island and received his degree in Music Performance from Duquesne University in Pittsburgh, PA. It was there that he began a lifelong passion for British Alternative music that burns through him to this day.

Still pursuing his passion to become a wanna-be Rock Music Historian like Nathan, T currently resides in the Central Florida area with his wife, Melissa, and their three boys Zac, Jordan, and Ben.

Learn more at www.tgamache.com.